Her Cross to Bear

HOUSE OF VAN HELSING BOOK 1

ERIN BEDFORD

ALSO BY ERIN BEDFORD

The Underground Series
Chasing Rabbits
Chasing Cats
Chasing Princes
Chasing Shadows
Chasing Hearts

The Crimes of Alice
The Crimes of Alice
Hatter's Heart
Cheshire's Smile

The Mary Wiles Chronicles
Marked by Hell
Bound by Hell
Deceived by Hell
Tempted by Hell
Betrayed By Hell

Starcrossed Dragons
Riding Lightning
Grinding Frost
Swallowing Fire
Pounding Earth

Curse of the Fairy Tales
Rapunzel Untamed
Rapunzel Unveiled
Rapunzel Unchained

Her Angels
Heaven's Embrace
Heaven's A Beach
Heaven's Most Wanted

DEDICATION

To my readers, who stuck with me through this crazy time.

HER CROSS TO BEAR

HOUSE OF VAN HELSING · BOOK 1

ERIN BEDFORD

CHAPTER 1

"NO WAY, THAT'S NOT even close to true!" I threw popcorn at the fake vampire on the television screen.

My dormmate and best friend, Bethany snorted beside me on her bed, our legs dangling off the edge. "How do you know what's true or not? Vampires could burst into dust." She threw a handful of popcorn into her mouth. "Look, it's an easy clean up."

I rolled my eyes. "Sure, but if a good gust of wind comes, all that dust is going right at you. Talk about second hand slaying." Not to mention all the politics and paperwork involved with killing a vampire, but Bethany didn't know that. Three years as roommates and there were tons of things Bethany didn't know about me.

"Second hand slaying? Really?" Bethany barked a laugh. "You are far too invested in vampire slaying for a premed student. Do they teach that stuff in Anatomy 302?"

I scooped up some popcorn and tossed it at her. "Hey, I can have other interests. There's no rule against it."

"Meh, sure. I guess." She gestured at the screen with a swooning sound. "Alive or dead, I'd let that British guy stick anything he wanted in me."

I wrinkled my nose. "Ew. Beth. He's the walking dead. He doesn't even have a heartbeat."

"Still, have you seen those abs?" She arched a blonde brow at me. "Lickable. Completely and totally lickable."

I giggled with her curling up closer on the bed.

Bethany had been my roommate and best friend since I started college. I loved her more than life itself but she could be so boy crazy. If she could get a glimpse of even half the men that I deal with back home, she'd orgasm on the spot. On second thought, it was probably better she didn't meet them.

In between episodes, Bethany smacked me on the shoulder. "Hey, what are we doing for your birthday?"

I grimaced, sticking my tongue out to the side. "Ugh. I have to go home for my birthday."

"What? Crysta, no." Bethany collapsed dramatically onto the bed. "Why would you want to celebrate your twenty-first birthday with a bunch of stuffy old farts?"

Forcing a grin, I shook my head. "It's fine. It's family tradition. I'm used to it." Not to mention, I'd turned twenty-one thirty-nine years ago.

"We have to celebrate when you get back." She grabbed me by the waist and hugged me close. "We just have to."

"No, no. It's fine." I told her, patting her on the back. "I'm not really into the bar scene."

Bethany leaned back and gaped at me. "I'm not talking about going to some dumpy bar. We have to go to a frat party. Do you know what kind of line up they'll throw for you?" She tugged on one of my long black curls. "You're like one of the hottest women at the school. Aside from me." She fluffed her blonde hair and winked.

"Of course," I smirked. "But I don't know about a frat party. They're kind of..." I trailed off trying to find a word that wouldn't offend her. "...stupid?"

Also, I didn't drink. In my line of work, being out of control was never a good thing. Even one drink could be the thing between life or death.

"Ugh, you're no fun." Bethany pouted and slid off the bed. "Fine. If you're determined not to let me get you blind out drunk, then you have to go to Cafe del Gato with me."

"What?" I groaned, glancing at the clock on her nightstand. "It's seven o'clock. I have a car coming for me at eight tomorrow."

"No, you don't," Bethany grabbed me by the arms and I allowed her to drag me off the bed. "We're going to get hopped up on expressos and go pet some pussy."

"Please don't call them that," I begged, shoving my feet into my boots. "They're cats. Not female genitalia."

"Ooh," Bethany cooed, wagging her brows. "You know what it does to me when you speak all medical."

"Come on, let's go. Before I make those vamp's deaths on T.V. look better than what I'm going to do to you."

After all, silver works so much better on vampires than wooden stakes. Everyone knows that.

We took the tram downtown, Bethany giggling the entire way about something that happened in her Economics class. I was only half listening. My eyes scanned the inside of the tram as they always did when I was out in public.

While I was playing the dutiful college student, I couldn't let go of my training. Fifty plus years of fighting the supernatural beings didn't just go away because I threw on a cardigan and backpack.

"And then Austin said, 'I don't make love, I make history,'" she burst into giggles, her head thrown back and mouth wide. It garnered her several looks from those around us. Which wasn't unusual, she was quite loud. Bethany didn't worry about drawing attention to herself, in fact, she reveled in it.

Me...not so much.

I didn't have that luxury. Keeping to the shadows had always been my goal. The moment they saw you coming that was when it was all over.

There.

The hair on my arm stood up. Discreetly, my eyes slid through the tram searching for what caused my skin to prickle.

A group of school girls chatted loudly, all of them crowded around one of the girls' cell phones. A baby cried as a young mother tried to calm it. The people around her giving her dirty looks. Assholes. A few college age guys were watching the school girls, their eyes meeting and leering smirks on their lips.

My gaze passed by a nondescript man. Then came back to him. There. It was him.

Shoulders stiffening, I inched closer to Bethany, placing myself in a protective stance around her as I surveyed the supernatural being.

Sensing supernaturals was my family's specialty. However, just because there was one near didn't mean I knew exactly what flavor they were on sight. This one could be a werewolf or a vampire or even an incubus for all I knew. He could be a witch's familiar too. It was hard to tell nowadays. It seemed like there were new/old creatures coming out of the woodworks every day.

This man had pale skin. Could be a vampire. Maybe an incubus. Nah. Not pretty enough. One thing I'd learned about the demons was they were hardcore about their looks. Like their siren calling magic wasn't enough to draw their victims in they had to look good too.

He must have felt my gaze on him. His eyes locked with mine and he huffed a laugh, flashing fang.

Vampire.

Bethany laughed again and bumped my arm. "Hey are you even listening to me?"

My eyes jerked away from the vampire to look at her. I smiled guiltily. "Sorry. No."

She turned to where I'd been looking. "What were you looking at?"

I followed her gaze, hoping she didn't notice the man. "Nothing. Just zoning out." I didn't have to worry. The vampire was gone.

Hopefully that would be the end of it. Unfortunately, my luck had never been that good.

"Thank fuck," Bethany sighed when we stepped off the tram and headed to the cafe. "I need a frap so bad right now."

"Yeah, I know what you mean." I tucked my hands into the pockets of my hoodie, my fingers curling around the small silver blade I had stashed there. Every shadow we passed was a potential hiding spot for an ambush. Had the vamp known what I was, then he might have thought twice about it. However, to the casual observer I was just another college girl hanging out with my friend.

Easy pickings.

"What?" Bethany snorted. "You never want coffee. Especially not this late."

I pulled my eyes away from the shadows. "Yeah, well, tonight I need it."

"Worried about visiting your family, huh?" Bethany looped her arm with mine and I almost told her to let me go. I didn't want her to get in the way if I had to fight. That would look suspicious though. If the vamp didn't know who I was, I didn't want to let him on to it.

I gave her a weak smile. "That obvious huh?"

Bethany laughed. "You can't hide anything from me. You're too tense. Like at any moment someone is going to drag you off and murder you."

I let out a nervous laugh. "Nope. You're a regular Sherlock Holms."

"Robert Downey Jr., not Benedict Cumberbatch."

Shaking my head, I scoffed mockingly, "Of course not."

"Ooooh, that cute guy is working the cash register today," Bethany squealed quietly, squeezing my arm. "Maybe he'll finally ask for my number today."

"Just ask him already." I pushed her forward a little bit wanting to be the last one in. "It's not like you to wait to be asked."

Bethany ran a hand through her silky blonde strands and giggled shyly. "Maybe I will."

Smiling at her back, I held the door open to the cafe and glanced back out behind me. No sign of the vamp so far. Though, that didn't mean much. He could be waiting for us on the way out.

The cat cafe, Cafe del Gato, had a periwinkle color scheme in the front cafe area and kind of a mass of colors in the back where the cats were locked in. You had to go through two sets of doors to get in so the little buggers didn't escape. We approached the cafe counter to order our drinks and pay our entry fee.

"Hey ladies, you're here late," the cute cashier, Ryan, pushed his glasses up his nose and grinned. "No parties to rave at tonight?"

Bethany giggled and flushed. "Oh no. We're not much into partying."

I gave her a sideways look. Really? This coming from the girl who had the best keg stand of them all. Bethany gave me a warning look. I pretended to zip my lips and looked back outside the large windows of the cafe. The streets were empty except for the occasional car that passed by. The street lights kept everything well lit and in the process creating just as many shadows.

After a bus passed by, a lone figure stood across the street. Arms crossed over his lean but muscular chest, the man wore a dark green button down silk shirt and tight black leather pants. He kept his dark brown hair slicked back and what I knew to be piercing blue eyes stared across the street at me. Those pouty lips quirked up on one side as if daring me to come out.

Xavier. The master vampire of the greater Midwest. What was he doing here?

"You know what you want, Crysta?" Bethany bumped me.

"Huh?" I turned away from the window and saw Ryan waiting for my order. "Uh...yeah. Just my usual." I took a step back, holding my phone up and eying Bethany, "I'll be right back, I need to make a call."

"But Crysta!" Bethany began with a whine.

"I promise. Real quick." I shook my phone. She sighed dramatically before turning back to Ryan. I darted out the door before she could stop me.

"Where the fuck are you?" I muttered to myself as I rounded the building and moved down the dark alley. My hand ducked into my hoodie pocket and I withdrew my blade. It wasn't big and wouldn't do me much good in a real fight but it was better than nothing.

As I inched down the alley, I began to think I had imagined it. Then I felt it. My hand shot out and grabbed the one inches from my shoulder. I leaned over at the same time I jerked on it, using my body weight to toss the perpetrator over me. Had I been a normal human this would be my time to run away. Since I wasn't, I didn't give the vampire a chance to retaliate. I lashed out at him. He was too fast, jumping out of the way before my blade could even touch him.

In front of me one minute and then gone the next. I spun around my heart racing as I searched for him. Something crashed into my back, shoving me against the brick wall of the building. I tensed as the body pressed against the back of mine, my hand clutching the dagger. The attacker didn't go for the kill, instead his hands slid down my arms, brushing along the sides of my breasts before settling on my hips, grinding his hard cock against my ass.

"Little girls shouldn't walk alone at night," a slightly accented voice crooned in my ear. "Someone could take advantage of them."

"Oh, yeah?" I smirked, turning my head to the side. "I think I can take care of myself." I swiped out with my dagger. It didn't get far before it was pinned in place, the stone biting into my hand until I dropped the weapon.

"Come again?" He ground against me once more.

I sighed, pushing my ass out against my better judgment. "What are you doing here, Xavier?"

Releasing my hands, Xavier spun me around so we were face to face. "Can't I have missed you?"

I arched a brow.

He laughed, a full throated sound that sent tingles in between my thighs. "Alright, perhaps not. However, when my fledgling mentioned sensing a hunter on the tram I couldn't help but come see you."

Understanding dawned on me. "Ah, so that was one of yours." I leaned my head back against the stone and stared up at him. "And here I thought I was going to have to hunt tonight."

"And now?" His hips swiveled against mine.

My lower lip pulled between my teeth as I hissed. "I can't. Bethany is waiting for me."

Xavier lowered his head until our lips were inches apart. "Tell her you got caught up."

Hands dropping from the wall to land on the firmness of his stomach. "I didn't exactly dress for a quickie."

He sniffed. "Has that ever stopped us before?"

"No." I barely got the word out before his lips crashed onto mine. My arms wrapped around his neck, fingers lacing into the soft strands of hair, completely messing it up. Xavier didn't care, he was much too busy searching every inch of my mouth. Fingers snuck beneath my hoodie, grabbing a fist full of my breast so tight that it pulled a sound from me.

I reached between us and pulled at the snaps of his pants. "No time for foreplay."

"I'll make up for it later," Xavier promised, pulling at my own pants. Luckily, I'd opted for sweat pants and not jeans. It made it easy to slip one pant leg off and throw it around Xavier's slender waist.

Xavier didn't hesitate before he shoved his impressive length inside of me. A burning sensation filled me as he worked himself inside. My head fell back and I gasped. It took no time at all before that tight fit turned into a slippery ride. The sound of skin slapping against skin echoed in the alley.

Someone could come by at any moment and see us. Which made it all the better. Even my best friend didn't know about these little rendezvous. And I liked it that way.

Eyes closing, I gripped onto his shoulders tightly, ruining the silk no doubt. Xavier didn't complain, his hips shifting back and then thrusting forward, bringing us both closer to that much needed release.

We never made love. It was always like this. Fucking. Sometimes it was quick other times, we took our time but it was the same every time. Both of us used the other to get what we wanted. I hardly remember how it started. A flirt here. A look there across the room at some supernatural gathering. Then a bloody misunderstanding turned into a quick and dirty romp in the gardens.

For twenty years, Xavier and I had never once told anyone about our little affair. Hell, we hardly admitted the fact to ourselves. We each had our own lovers over the years and yet in between, we always came back to one another. Some might say that meant something.

I wasn't so sure.

The one thing I did know for certain was that when he was inside of me, everything else melted away and I could just be. If it was the same for him I didn't know and didn't care to ask.

That crest came on fast as it did in quick fucks like this. Xavier knew it by now. The slight hitch in my breath. The quake in my legs and tightening of my fingers on his shoulders.

Xavier's mouth left mine and dipped between my shoulders. His fangs skimmed along the column of my neck, silently asking for permission. I angled my head to the side, giving it.

The sharp piercing pain on my neck set my orgasm over the edge. I clapped my mouth shut to keep back the scream threatening to leave my throat. My insides squeezed around Xavier's cock and I bucked against him trying to prologue the feeling. Once I returned home, I wouldn't have time to sneak in these little trysts. My father would make sure of that.

All too soon Xavier pulled away from my neck, blood seeping out the edge of his mouth. His tongue darted out and licked up the remnants of me. I'd be lying if I didn't admit that his hunger for me didn't turn me on even more. And if Bethany hadn't been waiting for me, I'd have gone another round or two with him just for good measure.

Alas...

I dropped my leg and let out a slow breath. It was signal enough for Xavier to realize we were done. He stepped back from me, adjusting his own clothing as I reached down to pull my pants back up. He'd long learned not to try to help me in any way. I wouldn't accept it even if he did.

Another attribute my father had ingrained in me. Van Helsings didn't need help from anyone. Least of all, lowly supernaturals.

There was a quiet tension between us that after twenty years one would think we'd have figured out how to leave without acting like total adolescents. Unfortunately, most of our encounters usually ended with Xavier saying something stupid that makes me get mad and leave in a huff.

"Your friend is tasty."

And here we go.

My eyes narrowed as I pulled my sweatpant strings a bit more aggressively than needed. "Stay away from Bethany."

Xavier smirked and rubbed his jaw line, his fangs flashing. "Bethany, mmm, I like that. Nice and adult."

I scowled, and shoved his shoulder. "I mean it. If you make me lose one of my only friends, I'll cut off your favorite part."

He clutched at his heart with one hand and mock gasped. "I thought I was your friend? And don't forget..." his expression warped as he snatched my hand and shoved it against his growing erection. "This is your favorite part too."

"Crysta?"

I jerked my hand back and whipped around. Bethany stood in the opening of the alley, a knowing gleam on her face. Great.

"Hey, Beth, sorry. I got held up." I hurried over to her side, not bothering to look back at Xavier.

Bethany stared over my shoulder with a wicked grin. "So, I see." She reached out and brushed at my hair. "You got some dirt there."

I flushed at being caught and quickly scraped at my hair, before grabbing her arm. "Come on, let's go before our coffees melt."

She followed me reluctantly before stopping. "Aren't you going to say goodbye to your..." she trailed off and gasped. "Woah, where'd he go."

Twisting around, I followed her line of vision to the empty alleyway. "Yeah, he does that." I tried to urge her forward again.

"That dude has some mad Batman skills," she murmured and I concurred silently. She had no idea.

CHAPTER 2

AS I STOOD IN the driveway of our dorm the next morning, I rubbed my eyes at the bright light and smiled weakly at Bethany, "I'll see you in a few days."

Bethany wrapped her arms around me in a tight hug. "You better message me every day. Let me know all the juicy aristocratic gossip." She wagged her brows at me mischievously.

Thankfully, she hadn't brought up my incident last night in the alley with Xavier. Though, she kept giving me curious knowing looks every time I looked her way. Not even the cute barista could distract her from me.

I patted her back and laughed. "Of course. Though, I doubt it will be too exciting. Like you said, a bunch of old farts." More like a bunch of immortals but still, not far off.

"Miss Helling," Gerald, my guard and constant pain in the ass, stood by the black sedan with the door open, waiting for me to get in. Gerald was hired muscle and he looked like it. Over six foot five with shoulders almost as wide as I was tall. The pale pink of his bald head shined in the morning sun as his watchful brown eyes stared at me and the surrounding area behind dark tinted glasses.

"Man, Crysta," Bethany whistled as she eye-fucked Gerald. "If my family sent someone who looked like him to guard me, I'd make sure I was in danger all the time." She winked and air kissed in Gerald's direction.

Gerald smirked.

"Don't let the monkey suit fool you, Beth," I told my friend, my eyes narrowing on Gerald in warning. "He's a thug and will break your heart before even learning your name."

Bethany curled her hair around her finger and giggled, cocking a hip to the side. "Oh, do tell. You know, I've always been a sucker for a bad boy."

I sighed and shook my head. She'd never learn. "Bad boys aren't all they're cracked up to be, believe me."

Bethany frowned at me. "I thought you didn't date much?" Then her brows lifted and her lips curved up. "Or are you talking about that hottie from last night because I could—"

"Okay, bye!" I interrupted her and turned toward the car. I waved at Bethany once more before climbing inside. Gerald closed it behind me and entered the front passenger side.

I let out a heavy sigh once I sank into the leather interior. I loved Bethany but keeping up my façade was more work than it was worth some days.

"Good morning, Miss Van Helsing." An elderly man with a kind smile and a driver's hat and gloves leaned over the driver's side.

I smiled at the driver. "Good morning, Lucas. Was the drive alright?"

Lucas had been with us since I was a child. Even before then. His family had served mine for as long as anyone could remember. He was one of the few humans who knew our secrets and kept them well.

We paid them handsomely for it of course. I'd like to think that they continued keeping our secrets out of loyalty and love rather than money. Though, I was sure the money didn't hurt either.

"Same as usual. Damn tourists can't figure out which side of the road they're supposed to be driving on." He chuckled cheerfully.

I laughed with him. "It never changes, I hear."

"Not many things do," Gerald murmured his two cents.

I shifted on the leather seats and relaxed back into them. "Home then?"

"I thought we might take the scenic route," Lucas replied, gesturing with his thumb to the back seat. "I assumed you would like to change before we arrived back at the estate?"

My eyes shifted to the garment bag, hanging beside me. Curious, I unzipped the bag and smiled. "Oh Lucas, you know me too well."

Withdrawing the black leather pants and soft white blouse, I jerked my sweater up and over my head, setting it on the seat beside me. I unsnapped my bra and let it fall to the floor without worry of Gerald or Lucas taking a peek. They feared my father far more than they wanted to eyeball my bare skin. Besides, both of them have known me since I was an infant. I would imagine it would be like watching one's niece undress.

Pulling the blouse over my head, I delighted in the feel of the fabric against my skin. Custom made clothing always felt better than the mass produced garments I wore for my human alias. My slacks went next as I expertly slid into the tight leather pants. It took a lot of practice dressing and undressing in the backseat of a car to get to the point where I was able to put leather pants on without strain. Many of these tales I could not regale my best friend with. She'd hardly believe me either way.

A red and black brocade over bust corset came next. Lacing one's corset required nimble fingers and practice, hours and hours of practice. Time I had happily spent.

Lastly, my ballet flats were exchanged out for a pair of heavy boots. I smoothed my hands over my new clothing and frowned. Something was missing. "Lucas, did you bring my—?"

"Underneath the seat, miss."

I bent down and reached under the seat. A length of leather straps and cold metal greeted my hand. With a happy sigh, I looped the leather through my belt loops and pulled the straps of the holster over my shoulders. The familiar heavy weight of the Colts pressed against the sides of my breasts.

I always felt so naked without them. Bringing them to school with me would cause suspicion and added danger to those around me. It was part of the agreement I had made with my father. If I was going to pretend to be human then I had to go all the way.

No weapons. No familiar clothing. No bodyguards to watch my every move.

Only Bethany knew that I came from a wealthy background and she'd only gotten it out of me after an intense game of truth or dare. I could have lied. I should have. Call me sentimental but I didn't want to lie to her. I wanted to give her some part of me that was real. Even if I couldn't give her more than that.

My phone dinged. I grinned. Speak of the devil.

I miss you already. Kiss a bunch of babies for me and by babies I mean Gerald's sexy head.

I snorted, shaking my head.

"Something funny, miss?"

"No, nothing." I tucked my phone into my purse and placed my human clothing into the garment bag. Sitting back in my seat, I settled in for the ride home.

It was safe to say I was not looking forward to returning home. As much as I missed my life, I enjoyed the uncomplicated ways of the humans. At home, there was so much to navigate. Every action, every word could be taken in so many ways. You could launch a war between species for the simple act of sneezing.

Well, not really, but you get the picture.

About ten minutes from home Gerald turned in his seat, a grim expression on his face. "I shouldn't even be telling you this but I want you to be prepared."

My brows furrowed. "Prepared for what?"

Gerald cleared his throat and shifted in his seat. "Well, you see. It's about your brother. Michael."

"What about him?"

My guard paused and turned his gaze out the window.

"We don't have enough road left for you to beat around the bush this much, sonny." Lucas snorted. It would be funny that he called Gerald, who was several centuries older than Lucas, Sonny had it not been for the pending news.

I leaned forward in my seat, my gaze darting between the two of them. "Someone tell me what's going on already?"

Gerald threw his hands up and sighed. "Michael is missing. This isn't just a party for your birthday. It's to announce you as the new Van Helsing heir."

"Excuse me?" I scoffed and wiggled a finger in my ear. "I must have something lodged in my ear because I thought I just heard you say that Michael is gone."

"Not gone, miss," Lucas corrected me. "Missing."

"Since when?" My mind whirled with the possibilities of what could have happened to my brother, my last living brother. I couldn't comprehend it. I couldn't handle losing another family member. We'd already lost my oldest brother Gabriel. Losing Michael too? That was just too much.

We were immortal for fuck's sake. Or mostly. Only the silver of our own weapons could kill a Van Helsing. It was one of our best kept secrets. So the likelihood of that happening was slim to none. Though, it obviously happens.

"Three months ago," Gerald explained gruffly.

I shot up out of my seat and bumped my head on the roof. "Three months!" I jerked back in my seat as Lucas came to a sudden stop in the driveway. "Why am I just hearing about this now?"

Gerald twisted in his seat, his eyes hard. "You wanted to live as a human, that means staying out of the family business. This is family business."

"But he's my brother," I snapped, my jaw clenched so tight it felt like it would break at any moment. "I should have been told. I would have come back—"

"That's exactly why you weren't told." Gerald quipped. "If you suddenly came back there would be questions and we weren't ready for anyone else to know until we had run out of options."

I swallowed thickly, the emotions building up in my throat. If they had run out of options that only meant one thing. They thought Michael was dead.

The gates of the Van Helsing estate sat before us. The moment Lucas reached the gatekeeper, they opened. He tipped his hat at Greg, another Van Helsing hired muscle, as we drove in.

About twenty years ago my father had finally paved the driveway. Until then, I always thought of the cracking of rocks beneath the car's tires as the sounds of home. Now it was just a silent smooth entrance. I missed the old sounds.

When Lucas drove around the circular driveway, he announced as he always did, "Welcome back home, miss."

As a child I had always been in awe of the Van Helsing estate. To someone small it might be confused as a castle. It wasn't. There was no princess at the top of the tallest tower. No prince waiting to ride in and save her. There was just me. I'd learned a long time ago that the only one who could save you was yourself.

To the outlooker the place would seem almost homey with its old fashioned brick and stone siding. The dark brown wood connectors gave it character that most homes did not have nowadays with their cookie cutter structure. White lined every inch of the three stories, four if you counted the little hideaway tower that I kept to myself.

The attempt at lightening the look of the estate didn't take away from the warding gargoyles on all four geographical corners. They were just as hideous and nightmare giving now as they had been when I was a child.

The building had been in our family since the 1800s, ever since my father decided to join the clans together as one house against the supernaturals.

Well, not necessarily against the supernaturals. My father would never be so blunt as to show his disdain for anyone not quite human. Even when he couldn't put himself completely in the human category. It still didn't keep Abraham Van Helsing from acting mightier than thou at every social gathering.

"Miss?" Lucas prodded and I realized I had been staring, Gerald already at my door holding it open as he waited.

I tossed him a grateful smile and stepped out of the car. I didn't bother taking my things with me. Lucas would make sure they were taken to my room for me. My father would have a fit if I came in with my hands full.

"A Van Helsing must always be prepared to fight. Never allow yourself to be compromised by carrying your own luggage."

The words had been hounded into me since I could understand them. I'd been waited on my entire life. It was second nature to me now. However, unlike my father and brothers who took their servants for granted, I always tried my best to make sure they were aware of my gratitude.

I peeked back in the car. "Thank you, Lucas. Say hello to your wife and son for me."

Lucas's eyes crinkled and waved me off.

My boots clicked on the pavement as I made my way up the drive and to the double dark mahogany doors. They opened before I even stepped a foot in front of them, opening up into the large entry way. Two sets of stairs lined either side of the entrance with a long balcony across the top. One would think it was for aesthetics but everything was a vantage point for my family.

From the way the windows were positioned just so that at least one always had the sun shining through to the way there was a mirror in every room. Even the plants were picked specifically to cover our scents from those nosey shifters. Nothing was done without forethought or a second meaning.

I stopped at the center of the entryway, staring up at the empty space. I wasn't put off by the lack of people waiting for me to return. I preferred it when no one made a fuss.

The rest of the Van Helsing clan were probably off doing their daily training or whatever it was that father had them doing. Perhaps killing off some of the more pesky demons. They'd no doubt make an appearance at the party tonight. A party that I had already not been looking forward to and now with the new news of my pending commencement, I was dreading the evening's events.

How would the supernatural world react to me? They had expected my brother, Michael, to take on the family legacy now that Father was retiring. Not that one could ever really retire from this life unless you were six feet under.

"Do you want me to ask the cook to send something up to eat?" Gerald asked from my side as I stared up at the ominous chandelier in the middle.

"Uh, no." I dropped my eyes and walked to the stairs. "I'll grab something later. I'm sure Father will want to speak to me. Give me the good news."

Gerald grimaced.

"Don't worry," I added before he could say anything. "I will act surprised and outraged as I was in the car. Your precious hide is safe."

His shoulders visibly relaxed.

For someone who had fought off vampires, werewolves, and demons on a regular basis, Gerald was far too afraid of my father. I suppose that's why we Van Helsings were in charge of making sure to keep the peace. Making sure the supernaturals didn't take over the world and make the humans their all you can eat buffets.

My fingers trailed up the stair rail as I took in my ancestral home. Paintings of Van Helsings who have long passed or were still alive today lined the walls. Each of them painted in that portrait way that made the eyes follow you as you passed. I even had one sitting in the main study alongside my brothers' and father's portraits.

Not my mother's though.

No. Hers was hidden away in father's room. I had a miniature of it in my own bedroom that I kept in the side table drawer. I took it out every once in a while to mull over what made her choose my father over all the humans she could have been with. Why him? Why a being that was more monster than man? If there were any redeeming qualities about Abraham, I had rarely caught sight of them.

I supposed he was loyal to the Van Helsings to a fault. Always putting Van Helsing's wants and needs above all others. No matter how much it might piss the supernaturals off. He had fought tooth and nail to make a place in this world for us and to keep the unsuspecting humans safe. So, I supposed that was a plus in his column.

I only wished he didn't step on so many on his way to achieving his goals.

My father had never been cruel. I couldn't call him comforting either. When I was five, my mother died of pneumonia and he had told me, "All things die if given enough time. Even us." That was all he had to say about it. I had to cry in the arms of Michael who spent the rest of the time trying to make me laugh. Gabriel was more like our father. Stern and almost robotic in his emotions. It was probably why it hurt more to lose Michael than it did him.

"Crysta!"

Holding back a groan of annoyance, I stopped in the hallway and put on a polite smile as I turned. "Eric, how are you?"

Eric Van Helsing, a cousin fifth remove or something of the like, irritated the crap out of me. It was nothing he did particularly. He just always seemed to be trying just a little bit too hard. His smile shined just a bit too bright and his answers to everything were just this side of too perfect.

One would call it jealousy. I called it precautious. No one was that perfect. Not without a reason to be.

He stopped before me in his dark jeans and button down shirt, his smile crinkling the edges of his cornflower blue eyes. Eric dragged a hand through his blonde hair, tousling it more than it already had been. "Oh, you know. Prepping for the party. You're coming right? It's in your honor after all."

I forced a smile. "Would Father let me do otherwise?"

Chuckling good natured, Eric shook his head. "Oh, yes. We cannot disappoint our great and powerful leader." He tucked his hands into his pockets and took up strolling next to me. "How was school?" Before I could answer he continued, "I wish my parents would have let me spend a year or two in the human world. Get away from all the life or death once in a while. It must be nice."

"Yep, nice and boring," I answered because he expected it.

"So, how are they?"

My brows furrowed. "How are who?"

He turned around so that he was walking backward as he talked, his hands behind his head. "Humans. What are they like?"

I pursed my lips. "You've met humans before, why are you asking me?"

Eric shrugged. "I don't know. I've met them in passing but I've never actually lived with one. Do they really all sleep a full eight hours?"

"If my roommate is the example, I'd say that is fairly under-exaggerated." Eric's eyes widened at my explanation. "She can sleep the whole day away if someone doesn't drag her ass out of the bed."

"No way!" He puffed out a breath of air. "I don't know how I could waste so much time. I mean, we're practically immortal but more than four hours and I'm itching to do something." He punched his fist into his other hand.

"Well, they don't have our stamina." I stopped at my bedroom door and turned away from him, ready to be done with the conversation.

"Yeah, I guess so." Eric grabbed my shoulder. "Hey, I wanted to tell you how sorry I was to hear about Michael. He was one of the best of us."

I stared at him. Was this a test? Was he trying to see if I already knew about it or was he really that stupid?

Eric's eyes widened and his mouth gaped as he realized his mistake. "Wait, did you not know...? Shit. Forget I said anything. I...I have to go." He darted away before I could stop him and reassure him that I already knew. Though, I suppose stopping him would only make him more upset and run to Abraham that someone had spilled the beans.

Oh, well. Nothing could be done about it now.

Safely behind my door, I leaned against it and sighed. The first of the many family members bound to bombard me with questions and condolences.

I needed to take this time while I could to get myself together. I couldn't fall apart in front of my father. Which was why I suspected Gerald had warned me.

Moving around my room, I took in the familiar sight. The four poster bed was a far cry from the twin bed I slept on back at the dorm. For some reason, the expansive room seemed colder and more lonely than the hole in the wall I shared with Bethany.

I opened the antique wardrobe on one side of the room and stared at the gown that sat waiting for me. A long skirt full enough that it puffed out when the doors opened greeted me. The material was the color of midnight and shone like the stars. Its bodice had a modest heart shaped neckline that wouldn't show off more than a hint of cleavage.

The gown was gorgeous of course. It just wasn't something I'd have chosen for myself. My tastes ran more on the simple and more accessible side of fashion. If I couldn't run in it, then I didn't want it.

My father might be more progressive when it came to having females fight and rule but he still insisted I dress like a lady. I couldn't fight him on this, not now. Not with Michael missing.

Blowing a breath out between my teeth, I closed the wardrobe and walked over to the balcony. I couldn't delay seeing Father for much longer. The party was tonight and he'd no doubt want to talk about what was going to happen and enlighten me to the situation before then. The question was when.

I pushed the balcony doors open and stepped into the fresh air. The house never felt so stifling as it did in that very moment.

Why? Why did it feel like the walls were closing in around me? Walls that had always felt too open, too vulnerable, now made my skin tight and my pulse race.

My fingers curled around the edge of the stone railing as I glared down at the grounds below. My breaths came in quick pants. I couldn't seem to get enough air in.

It was hot. Why was I so hot?

I tugged at my corset and lifted my hair off my neck. Oh God. This was really happening. Michael was gone and I was going to be the head of the Van Helsing clan. I was going to be in charge. Me.

Fucking hell.

I couldn't do this. I couldn't be trapped here until I turned into my father. My gaze dropped to the bushes below. It wasn't that far of a jump. I probably wouldn't even break a bone. I could leave now. Find Bethany. She'd help me disappear. Help me live as a human. I wouldn't have to be the heir. I could leave right now—

A knock on my door brought me back to Earth.

I took a long deep cleansing breath and shook myself out.

No. I couldn't. As much as I wanted to leave all the responsibility behind and just be a human, I couldn't. Who would run the clan in my place? Eric? One of my other relatives? They were as bad as my father, if not worse. Wanting to put more regulations on the supernaturals making them basically second class citizens. While the other side wanted to give them more freedom and let them run wild on the humans.

I had to be the balance. I had to bear this cross because there was no one else who could do it.

"Crysta?" The voice of my favorite cousin, Ines, called out. "You going to hide in there all day?"

I hurried across the room and opened the door, enveloping her in a tight hug before she could say anything else. Breathing in the smell of the coconut oil she used basically for everything, I let myself have a moment to just relax. Her hands came around to settle on my back automatically, holding me just as tightly.

She wasn't really my cousin at least not in the sense that humans thought of cousins. Our clan was made up of many members and while we have integrated between ourselves over the hundreds of years we've existed the lines had become so blurred that keeping track was almost impossible.

When I didn't let go right away, Ines murmured into my ear. "You heard, didn't you?"

I pulled back, untangling my hands from her long multicolored braids as I swiped at the wetness on my face. "Gerald told me in the car."

Understanding crossed her face and she quickly closed the door behind her. Grabbing my hands, she held them tight. "I wish I had told you sooner but your father—"

I cut her off, shaking my head. "I understand why you didn't. I'm just sorry I wasn't here with you. We could have worried together."

Ines smiles weakly. "But you're his sister. You should have known."

"And you're his fiancé. You couldn't have told me even if you wanted to. No outside influence, remember?" I reminded her as the image of Xavier in the alleyway flickered into my mind. I pushed it away and dragged her into my embrace again. Her smaller frame made it so I was easily able to lay my chin on top of her braids. "Please don't think anymore of it. And besides, he's not dead. Just missing."

Ines jerked back. "You don't think he's..."

My jaw tightened. "Until I see a body, I won't give up searching for him. No matter what Abraham thinks."

Ines' eyes watered and she collapsed against me. "I knew I could count on you. I knew you weren't going to let them walk all over you."

I patted her back. "Don't worry. We'll find him and make the devil's who took him pay in blood."

CHAPTER 3

INES WALKED WITH ME until I stopped outside of my father's study, then she left to help prepare for the party, leaving me to face my father alone.

I lifted a hand and knocked on the hard wooden door. I didn't enter until I heard his muffled voice giving me permission. Abraham ingrained his privacy onto us as children. We were never allowed to come to him at night when we had bad dreams. Not unless we wanted a lecture on why we were more feared than any pretend monster.

He said it was to teach us self-reliance and strength. The same reason was given for any other parental task he didn't want to do.

If we were sick there was a doctor in the house who could take care of us. If we fell down and bruised our knee we got back up and kept going. A Van Helsing was never weak. Never needed outside help. Even from their own parents.

Stepping into the office, a rush of claustrophobia tried to overcome me again. I drew in deep breaths and forced myself to move forward.

The walls were full of shelves with books from ancient lore to the more current reports. My father wanted to be prepared for anything. Even if it were make believe.

"Who knows what our enemies will use against us?"

My mother's portrait sat behind his desk above the mantel surrounded by two silver swords engraved with a VH on each handle. They were his original weapons against the creatures of the dark. He rarely got his hands bloodied anymore though so they sat there on the wall, silent guardians to my mother's image.

I looked like her or that's what I was told. I didn't see it. We had the same curly black hair and brown green eyes but my sharp nose came from Abraham and the disappointed sneer that lined his lips I had also seen on my own face. I didn't remember if she was as tall as me and my father was a few inches taller than my five foot nine height. So I could only imagine.

"Why didn't you come to see me right away?" My father didn't even glance up from the papers in front of him and still his voice held the commanding tone of a king.

"I wanted to see my room." I stepped up to the desk but didn't sit down.

He snorted. "It hasn't changed has it? I will have the maid fired if anything has been touched."

"No," I quickly replied. "It's the same." I paused and when he didn't add anything I commented, "I saw my gown for this evening. It's lovely."

Still his gaze did not lift. "Good, then you won't argue with me about leaving those tacky things behind."

My hands immediately went to my Colts. Father always preferred swords to guns and had no qualms about letting everyone know it.

I knew better than to get offended and argue with him. He wouldn't change.

Abraham Van Helsing was as unchanging as his looks. He hadn't in the five hundred years he had ruled the Van Helsing clan. Why would he change now? Which was why it was so surprising to hear he wanted to retire a few years ago. Michael and I had looked forward to not having Father as the head of the clan. To finally have some freedom to just be. Except now it looked like it would be me making that happen.

My father didn't say anything else. I waited with my heart hammering in my chest for him to mention Michael. For him to tell me he was dead or missing. To tell me that it all depended on me now.

He didn't. Instead, he glanced up from his work and frowned. "Well, don't waste your day here. Go get ready."

Shocked by his dismissal, I automatically turned on my heel and made for the door. My hand touched the doorknob, curling around the cool metal before I dropped my hand and asked in a low voice, "Were you ever going to tell me?"

"What's that? Look at me when you're speaking. You are aware my hearing isn't what it used to be."

I scoffed and spun on my heel, marching across the room to slam my hands on the top of his desk. The items shifted, a knickknack of a wolf falling over on its side. "When were you going to tell me that Michael is missing?"

Father took his time righting the little wolf before lifting his gaze to mine. I expected to see pain, anger, irritation, some kind of reaction to my outburst. Instead all I saw was a weariness that hadn't been there before. Or maybe it had and I'd never noticed? Either way, I needed answers and I would get them.

"I assumed someone else would tell you before we had a chance to talk and it would appear that I was correct." He pushed back from the desk and stood. Hands shoved into his pockets he walked to the side of the room, his gaze lifting and turning back to the portrait of mother. "She never wanted this for you, you know. She took solace in the fact that your older brothers would bear this cross and that you never would."

I watched as he paused for a moment, taking a deep breath before turning to me. For the first time in my fifty plus years of life, a look of regret crossed my father's face. However, it was gone as soon as I blinked.

"Unfortunately, things do not always work out how you planned." His face grew serious. "The Van Helsing clan is now your cross to bear. I know you will serve it well and understand the hazards behind having this position considering your condition."

I swallowed and licked my lips, nodding. "Yes. I understand."

He nodded and turned from me.

Taking it as a dismissal, I pivoted for the door. This time it was my father who stopped me.

"I'll have Gerald gather your belongings from school. We'll begin your training immediately after tonight's events."

My fingers curled into tight fists as I bit out, "Yes, father."

I forced myself not to slam the door behind me as I escaped into the hallway. Keeping my feet moving, I didn't stop even when other members of the house greeted me. My eyes forward, I stalked down the steps and past the bustling servants working on making the house presentable for tonight. I scoffed at the thought.

Like the supernaturals cared what our home looked like. They'd hate us all the same if we had dust or moths.

"Miss Van Helsing your father instructed -" a maid, Catherine, who usually helped me prepare for these events tried to cut me off but I brushed her aside with a scorching glare. She gasped and bowed her head to me. "I'll wait in your room then."

Immediately, I felt bad for letting loose my anger at my father on her. However, she had run off before I could apologize. I'd do it later. After I sweated off the need to rip my father's head off with my bare hands.

The training room door slammed against the wall as I stalked in. The sound reverberated through the room and the others who were training paused in their activities.

My eyes searched the room for something to punch. As luck would have it, Jerrod, my second favorite Van Helsing walked toward me.

"If I know you at all, you just spoke with your father." Jerrod grimaced, crossing one muscular arm over the other so his chest muscles bulged. It wasn't a purposeful flaunt of his body; he was just that big. It made me feel better about kicking his ass.

"Get in the ring," I ordered, moving to the side to remove my shoulder holsters and wrap my hands. Normally for training I'd keep them on. No use fighting without the equipment and then going into battle for real and floundering over the extra weight and restraint.

Today, though, I wanted freedom to move how I wanted. I wanted to be able to pulverize something into the ground without having to worry about the urge to shoot them.

No. Having my Colts was too tempting for my state of mind now.

Jerrod didn't argue or complain about my orders. He simply wrapped his hands and climbed into the training ring we had off to one side of the room. The rest of the training area was a mixture of dummies and targets for using weapons and perfecting fighting moves without an opponent. The ring though. The ring was meant to put those moves into practice. It was probably why the floor mat was blood red to hide the amount of beatings that were given here.

Jerrod was my cousin in some way. Most of the Van Helsings could follow their lineage back to someone being related to someone from somewhere. However, at some point we had to bring in new blood or we'd end up with too pure of blood and a stupid hunter was a dead hunter. Dalliances with humans were actually encouraged however relationships were not. Usually, Van Helsing's blood was strong enough to make sure all the children turned out to be immortal like us.

Well, except for one.

"So, what did dear old Abraham have to say?" Jerrod asked as I lunged at him.

I swung left and he dodged right. Gritting my teeth, I growled, "Nothing I didn't already know."

Jerrod chuckled, flicking his head so that his almost dark brown hair got out of his face. "You wouldn't have that murderous look in your eyes if that were true." He leaned into my next hit before dropping to the ground to sweep my legs out from under me.

I hit the mat hard enough to jar my teeth. Rage pulsated through my body making my blood pump faster and my movements quicker. When Jerrod approached, thinking he had won no doubt, I grabbed him by the leg, swinging my other to hit his knee knocking him to the mat. I twisted my body around him until I had him pinned beneath me, his arms and legs useless in my hold.

Jerrod grunted and tried to get up, but I kept him in place with a small amount of pressure on his joints. "Fine. I give." He sighed and dropped his head back.

A roar of applause and laughter filled my ears. Glancing up to the audience around the ring, I pursed my lips and rolled my eyes. Children, the lot of them.

I pushed off of Jerrod and offered him a hand up. He took it.

"What was it this time Jerrod?" Another cousin, I wasn't sure what number, called out to him, a grin on her face. "Ten seconds? I think you're getting worse."

Jerrod flipped her off. "I'd like to see you do better, Mandy."

The others around her chortled and egged her on, trying to get her to fight me.

Giving the poor girl a break, I held my hands up and shook my head. "Maybe another time. I have to get ready for the party."

A round of boos and disappointment filled the training room.

I turned my back on them and worked on unwrapping my hands, Jerrod following after me.

"So...?" He trailed off acting as if he hadn't just had his ass handed to him.

"So what?" I answered back being obtuse on purpose.

"What'd your dad say?"

I sighed. "Nothing. Absolutely nothing. He left it to others to tell me my brother was missing."

Jerrod snorted and dragged a hand through his hair as he shook it. "That's typical Abraham for you. Letting others do his dirty work."

I huffed a laugh. "He did find the courage to tell me I was the new heir."

"You mean, he actually said it like it was a good thing?" Jerrod made a face with his tongue. "No one in their right minds would want to be the heir. We're lucky Michael was insane enough to take on the job."

"Yeah," I frowned and stared down at the tiled floor as we walked through to the kitchen. "Honestly, I think it was more of a warning not to embarrass him and that my charade as a normal human girl was over."

I grabbed an apple off the kitchen island and waved at Ana, the main cook, while she ordered the others around. Before I could get out the door with my apple, she called out, "Stop right where you're at!"

I froze in the doorway, my apple stuck in between my teeth.

"Jerrod Patrick Van Helsing," Ana growled, marching over to us. "What did I tell you would happen if you touched one single crumb of the food for tonight?"

I pulled my apple out of my mouth, crunching the bite and glancing over at my cousin.

Jerrod had his mouth clamped shut and his hands behind his back, his eyes wide with fear.

Besides my father, the only one who could strike fear in the hearts of us hunters was Ana. She controlled the kitchens. If you got on her bad side you'd be stuck fending for yourself for a week.

Jerrod swallowed hard, his eyes watering as he gasped, "I didn't touch any of them, I swear."

"Lying and thieving now, are we?" Ana tapped her foot, her hands fisted on her round hips. Her pale almost milky blue eyes narrowed on him, daring Jerrod to dig a deeper whole.

My lips quirked to the side though wisely kept my mouth shut.

Thankfully, Jerrod did too. He withdrew his hands from behind his back and bowed his head, handing over the cherry turnover he'd snagged.

Ana snatched it up and waved it at him, crumbs flying everywhere. "You best be thankful tonight is mandatory for all of the primary hunters or you'd be getting no dinner tonight. Now what do you have to say for yourself?"

Jerrod's large shoulders curled in on themselves as he tried to make his six foot five form as small as possible in front of the five-two cook. "Sorry, Ana."

A snort of laughter escaped my nose and those stern eyes whipped over and landed on me. "And you, young lady. Miss 'I'm the heir now I don't have to worry about my health'? Did you think I'd let you sneak out of here with just an apple? Have you had a real breakfast yet?"

I opened my mouth to answer.

"I'll take that as a no, since your father thought he was more important than filling your belly." Ana grabbed me by the arm and dragged me further into the kitchen. Pushing down on my shoulders, she forced me to sit at the little table in the corner. "Now you sit here and eat something with some protein in it." Ana opened the fridge and grabbed a plate of sandwiches, setting it down on the table in front of me.

Jerrod eye balled the sandwiches while I bit into one. The moment he took a step forward, Ana shot him a look.

"Not you. You get out of my kitchen before I convince Abraham he needs more hunters on patrol tonight."

Jerrod's eyes widened and without a goodbye darted out of the kitchen.

Ana bustled around the kitchen more, ordering trays moved, tasting things in pots, and generally keeping the ship going. She had run the kitchens for as long as I could remember. Even when my brothers were children. And yet she didn't look a day over twenty-five. Van Helsings could chalk it up to good genes. Really it was the gypsy magic that kept us ageless. We'd never die of old age. Never grow old and grey with our grandchildren all around our deathbed.

The only object that could kill a Van Helsing was that of our own making. A blessing and a curse. Many Van Helsings had gotten tired of their immortal life and had put a silver blade through their heart or bullet in their brain. It was another reason my father was so against any of us getting involved with humans. Too many lost loves to the master of all things...time.

If my father ever mourned my mother to the point of wanting to end his own life, I'd never know. He sure didn't act like it. Though, I'd catch him every once in a while just staring at her portrait. So, I do know he loved her but how much?

"I was sorry to hear about your brother." Ana sat down across from me at the table, her hands grasping my free one. My other hand held the half eaten sandwich I'd forgotten about in my thinking.

"Thank you," I laced my fingers with hers and squeezed it. "All is not lost though. I will find him."

Ana gave me a small smile, almost pitying. "I'm sure you will. Now eat up. I know you'll have your hands full tonight and won't likely get another chance to eat before bed."

I bit into my sandwich to make her happy though it rolled in my stomach. Tonight. Tonight my father would announce to the supernatural world I was the new heir to the Van Helsing clan. Tonight everything would change. Perhaps not for the better.

CHAPTER 4

I FELT CLAUSTROPHOBIC AGAIN. Even with the large ballroom spread out before me, the walls never felt closer. The high ceiling with its gaudy gold and diamond chandelier pressed down on me. Between each stone pillar stood a set of glass paned doors leading out into the gardens. Except they might as well be nonexistent for how small they had gotten in my hysterics. Every exit and person pushed closer and closer around me until I saw spots behind my eyes.

Squeezing my eyes shut, I curled my fingers into a fists until the nails bit into my palms. The pain helped. I swallowed and smoothed the dress down my body for what had to be the tenth time in the last five minutes.

I could do this. It wasn't like they were all down there in the ballroom - waiting for me. They were waiting for my father too.

The head of each supernatural clan and their entourage had come tonight. While the Van Helsing clan would be out in full force, the supernatural clans were only allowed to bring a dozen people with them. This included the head of each clan and their guards if they so chose to bring them. It was a flaunt of strength. A power play. My father always had to make sure they knew their place. Beneath our boots.

It made tonight all the more nerve wracking. The supernatural community would look to me now. Wondering if I would control them with an iron fist the way my father did or give them more leeway. Tonight would only be the beginning of the negotiations and ass kissing from the other clans hoping to get in my good graces.

I'd never been good at the game. My father had made sure to keep me out of the spotlight as much as possible. He couldn't have any of the supernaturals learning about my condition. It was even more imperative now that I'd be the face of the clan.

"Calm yourself," my father reprimanded me in a hushed tone. "You must never let them know how you are feeling. Emotion is -"

"Weakness," I completed for him with a huff. "Yes, I know." Then muttered to myself, "You'd be nervous too if you were suddenly on the chopping block."

"What was that?" Abraham adjusted his cufflinks without looking at me.

"Nothing." I took a deep breath and plastered a confident smile on my face. "Just saying how much I'm looking forward to this."

"Well don't let them know it." He stepped toward the edge of the balcony and glanced over the railing at the crowd below. "They're like leeches, just waiting for the first hint of blood before they attack." He turned back to me with a stern look. "Always be on your guard."

I nodded my head dutifully and waited until he had taken his place at the staircase before stepping forward as well, standing a bit behind him.

A hush came over the crowd below as he stepped onto the stairs. His presence alone was enough to fill the room. My father stopped at the bottom of the steps and said in a booming voice, "My friends, I am pleased you have all come on this most auspicious of nights. My retirement!" There was no cheering or whooping. They wouldn't dare. A polite round of applause barely broke the air. My father grinned arrogantly, "As all good things come to an end, we must not see this time as a time for mourning but for celebration because as I go, I will be leaving the Van Helsing clan and the supernatural community in more than capable hands."

My heart thudded in my chest so hard and fast in my chest I was sure they could hear it down below.

This was it.

The first step into the life my father had laid out for me. The life that should have been Michael's. My mind raced back to a conversation I'd had with my brother.

"Don't worry so much, Crys." Michael said, ruffling my hair. "Father would never put you in harm's way. Why do you think he lets you run around in the human world and not be a hunter full time?"

"But it's not fair." I scowled, crossing my arms and stomping my foot like a child. "I want to fight, not stand in the shadows."

Michael laughed. "If the sups found out one of us was half human, what do you think they would do?"

"What does it matter?" I argued for the hundredth time. "I can do everything a full fledged Van Helsing can do. I should be out there policing the supernaturals with you." I shot toward him without warning, hoping to catch him off guard and finally win against him.

To my dismay, Michael was ready for me. His dagger was out and pressed against the pulse of my neck within moments, causing me to freeze in place. A stinging sensation made me hiss as liquid slid down my throat.

"See, Crys. You're not like the rest of us." He slowly removed his blade and held it up so I could see the blood staining the side. "My blade shouldn't have been able to pierce your skin and yet it did."

I glared at the knife as if it was to blame for my human weakness.

Michael sighed. "You will be much happier if you accept who you are and the limitations that come with it. I know I would sleep better at night if you did."

I snorted. "Limitations are meant to be overcome. I won't be told what I can and cannot be by someone who's not me."

Michael stared at me for a long moment before nodding. "Very well. I'll plead your case to father but don't say I didn't warn you. The hunter's life will be even harder for someone with a secret such as yours, I pray you won't regret it."

My eyes watered as I pushed the memory back. I didn't regret it. Not one second of my time hunting. What I did regret was not being here when he was taken. I might be part human but Van Helsing blood ran through my veins and I wouldn't stand idly by and let my father do whatever he wished. I would find Michael, starting with the room of suspects below.

"Unfortunately, my son Michael has fallen while out on a deadly mission. However, my daughter, Crysta, is more than willing to help us move forward into this new day and age."

The fuck I am.

Curling my fingers into a fist, I took a deep breath before blowing it out and plastering a neutral expression on my face. My sides felt bare without my Colts strapped to them even with all of the fabric covering my body. The skirt swished against the stairs with every step I took. I focused on the sound of it as my eyes trailed the crowd.

Ines stood near father waiting for any sign of trouble. Jerrod had to be somewhere in the crowd as well. Focus Crysta. Focus.

Step. Swish. Vampires. Step. Swish. Succubi. Step. Swish. Shifters - wait...where were the shifters?

For a brief moment, my mask broke. My lips curved down in a frown and my brow scrunched together. Then my eyes locked onto a familiar face in the crowd - Xavier.

The master vampire wore his signature silk shirt and tight pants as he stood amongst his entourage. A mixture of vampires I had only briefly seen in passing. The one I'd seen the other night with Bethany stood close to Xavier's side, a bored expression on his face.

Xavier shifted, drawing my attention back to him. He lifted his hand and blew me a kiss. To anyone else it would be seen as a mocking gesture but to me, someone who was intimate with the vampire on a regular basis, it was a reminder.

People were watching. I wasn't free to react however I wanted here. I pushed my face back into the mask required of me and continued down the staircase.

My father waited at the bottom of the steps and to the untrained eye would seem as if he were a doting father patiently waiting for his child. However, I saw the wrinkle in his brow, the tightening of his jaw. He was not pleased with my distraction.

Well, tough.

If I was to be the new head of the Van Helsing clan then things were going to go my way. Not Abraham's. His time was over.

When I reached the bottom of the steps my father offered out his arm to me. I reluctantly took it, knowing the warning that would come with it.

"Remember, you have no friends here." The harsh whispers of his words were barely loud enough for me to hear.

He was wrong. I had many friends here. It was my father who had put a wall between himself and the supernaturals. And while he had done his best to keep me away from the spotlight shoving my brothers into it at every turn that had only made many of the supernaturals in this room more curious about me. It was what caused Xavier and several others to seek me out the first time.

"Ah, little Crysta Van Helsing," Xavier purred, taking my hand in his as soon as I was within reach. "You have grown into such a delectable morsel." I fought to roll my eyes while Xavier overplayed our meeting for my father and the others. His lips brushed the back of my hand in a completely proper kiss and then twisted our hands so that my wrist was to the air. His tongue lapped along my pulse in a slow sensuous dance before my father could object. As Xavier wanted, my pulse jumped and hot liquid pooled between my thighs, scenting the air.

"You overstep your bounds, Xavier," my father warned, stepping close enough to force Xavier back.

The look Xavier gave me was not innocent. It said exactly what he wanted to do to me there in the middle of the ballroom with everyone watching. A part of me wanted him to do it as well. However...

I threw my head back and laughed, refusing to let myself be embarrassed by the fact that every single person in the room could smell my desire. My laughter put Xavier and several others off kilter. My father stood confused by my reaction.

Withdrawing my hand from Xavier's, I stared at where he had licked me and mused aloud, "And I thought it was only the succubi who could elicit such a reaction. Or perhaps it is just your natural charms? What do you think?" I cocked my head to the side, daring him to push me further.

Xavier held his hands up and stepped back, a clear sign that he was withdrawing his challenge to me. "You flatter me, Miss Van Helsing. I am but a humble vampire. I may look young but once you've lived several centuries, you will understand."

His fellow vampires chuckled around him good-naturedly. The Van Helsings guards assigned to my father and I were tense and closing in. No one seemed to know how to react to our little exchange. Except my father.

"Well, I am pleased to see you two getting along so well." My father glanced between the two of us. If he was suspicious he didn't show it. "Please enjoy the rest of the evening. We must greet our other guests."

My father tightened his grip on my arm and led me away from the still chuckling vampires. I shot a warning look behind my father's back at Xavier who only winked in return.

Asshole.

We strode purposefully across the ballroom past the empty space the shifters were supposed to occupy. I held back asking about them in front of so many ears and focused on the group ahead of us.

Where the vampires wore a variety of clothing from this era and others, the succubi held themselves to a different standard. Clad in designer clothing worth no less than a few thousand a piece, they would have looked more at home on the red carpet than here in our ballroom. Their leader, Elise, wore a silvery almost sheer dress that clung to every inch of her voluptuous curves. Her golden hair fell down her back in elegant waves, brushing against her backside as she moved.

I kept my eyes on her lovely face and tried to ignore the fact that her nipples were blatantly visible through the thin straps of material covering her breasts. When my father and I stopped before her, she giggled. The sound like a gentle caress along my skin causing my own nipples to pebble and the heat that had cooled between my thighs to reignite.

"Enough, Elise," my father demanded.

"But Abraham," Elise's plump lips pushed out into a pout. She sashayed toward my father and pressed her full form against his side. I released his arm, fighting the urge to show my disgust. "The vampires tried to do it first. You cannot blame me for wanting to prove we are still the rulers of seduction."

She batted long black lashes over her emerald green eyes and wiggled against my father's side.

I thought I was going to be sick.

"Please excuse my mother," a smooth tenor voice brushed along my ear. Slowly, I turned toward the most beautiful man I'd ever seen in my fifty-nine years of life. Hazel eyes peered down at me with such intensity, I found myself blushing without meaning to. Perfectly pouty lips, not unlike Elise's, curved up into a lopsided grin.

The man - no incubus - had the most symmetrical face in existence. Even the shaved sides of his head were perfectly aligned. The longer dark blonde hair stylishly put in place matched the coloring of his brows and the scruff along his square jawline. Not a single inch of him wasn't meant for seduction. From the tailored suit covering his masculine yet slender body, to the tattoos covering every exposed inch of him except that gorgeous face.

I found my mouth hanging open as I took him completely in. Another sultry giggle from Elise snapped me out of it. I clamped my mouth shut and took a step back from the tempting patchouli and cedar scent wafting into my nose and skin.

Damn these demons.

Unlike vampires who were human once upon a time, the succubi were never human to begin with. No one knew for sure where they came from originally. Hell, space, the primordial ooze, it didn't really matter. They were here and they were here to stay. The trick was not to get sucked into their 'gifts' as they called them. Succubi weren't completely like they were told about in mythology. While they can and do feed off their victims' life force, they couldn't accidentally kill you. There had to be a purpose behind it. This incubus wasn't trying to kill me or I'd have been incapacitated already. He was trying to test me though.

I locked eyes with the man and plastered a smile on my face that was not at all pleasant, my fingers sliding into the hidden slit of my skirt. "I would advise against using your wiles against me in future encounters."

The man took a step closer, my father and Elise only watching from the sides, as he cupped the side of my face. "My apologies, little Van Helsing. I did not mean to offend. Please, let's be friends."

His power rushed across my skin and caused a gasp to escape between my lips. My hand which had found the butt of my Colt strapped to my thigh kept me from getting caught up in his game. Within a blink of an eye, I had the Colt out and the barrel shoved against the ribs of the gorgeous man.

He froze, his eyes widening. With how close we were no one could see my actions but they knew something had happened by the way his entourage and our guards stepped forward. His eyes darted to the sides and I saw on his face when he made the decision.

Just like his mother, he threw his head back and laughed, a sound that reverberated to my very core. I tightened my hand on the butt of my Colt even harder until my bones ached.

"It's fine. It's fine. It's my fault for pushing, Miss Van Helsing." Glancing down at the Colt against him, the incubus cocked his head to the side. "Can I move?"

My finger ached to pull the trigger, I forced it to relax against the side of the barrel as I bit out, "Slowly."

When he moved far enough back that everyone could see my gun, a silent tension went through the room. Except my father who only chuckled darkly.

"That's my Crysta for you," He removed Elise from his person and clamped a hand on my shoulder, the grip so tight I fought back a wince. "She has her mother's temper. I wouldn't tease her so, Azeryth."

The incubus before me, scratched the back of his head and huffed a laugh. "My apologies, Abraham. I didn't mean any harm."

"Of course," my father inclined his head and then looked down at me. "I believe you can put your weapon away now, daughter." The tone of his voice told me we would be having a discussion later about how I'd defied his orders to come unarmed. I ignored it. He should know more than anyone that someone in my position could never be completely vulnerable. Not unless I wanted to die.

Still, I obeyed his order and slid the pistol back into its holster on my leg, smoothing the skirts back into place. The tension in the room didn't lower though as we moved away from the succubi. Normally, we would go to the shifters next and yet they were nowhere to be seen. Someone else had obviously noticed their absence and would say something wouldn't they? I couldn't wait any longer to question my father about it.

I turned to him and opened my mouth, "Father, where are -"

Glass shattered on all sides of the room and a burst of wind showered the guests with the broken glass. Screams filled the ballroom as everyone tried to cover themselves from being cut. The Van Helsings hurried in front of the guests since normal glass couldn't harm them. My father grabbed me by the arm and jerked me behind him. He was too late.

CHAPTER 5

A STINGING PAIN LACED through my hand. I shoved it beneath my skirt in the pretense of grabbing my gun to hide the cut. Now would be the worst time for everyone to find out my weakness.

The Van Helsing guards scrambled to get between my father and myself, doing their duty to protect us from the intrusion. I found myself surrounded by Eric and Ines, one making me relax while the other making my skin crawl. It was a peculiar feeling that I didn't have time to contemplate.

"You okay there, cousin?" Eric asked, his brows furrowed as he glanced down at me.

I shoved my hand further beneath my skirt, trying to hide my bloodied hand though I could feel the blood slip down my fingers and onto the floor.

Thankfully, I wasn't the only one who had been hit by the glass shards. While the Van Helsing could be injured by weapons other than their own, they healed quite quickly. Not fast enough that blood didn't seep to the surface which helped in my favor. If it had only been my blood in the air, there would be more questions than we would want to answer. We had bigger problems right now.

The shrieks of the succubi overcame most of the noise from the intruders and guards. They of course cared far more for their appearance than anyone else in the ballroom. They scrambled to attend to their queen who had been cut in several places. Her son who had been near me, miraculously didn't have a single mark on him and kept curiously looking in my direction.

I forced my attention away from him and focused on what was happening around me. The vampires had been far enough away from the spray of glass that if they had any injuries they weren't complaining. The scent of blood in the air caused their eyes to light with hunger and their fangs to peek between their lips.

"We should get the vampires to a different room," I mentioned to whoever would listen. Which ended up being Eric since my father had conveniently ended up a few yards before me with his guards.

"I'll have Torres urge them -"

Ines snorted. "You mean piss them off. Torres has all the tact of a rhino. I'll get the vampires fed before they start feasting on the succubi. You stay with Crysta." She patted my bare shoulder and gave me an encouraging smile before moving toward the salivating supernaturals.

"Guess, it's just you and me, eh cousin?" Eric tried to make light of the situation.

I didn't return his forced grin. I was far more interested in what was happening before us.

The guards seemed to have figured out that whoever had busted through the glass was not a threat. The crowd of them spread like locusts that had just devoured a feast. I angled to see around the moving bodies without being too obvious. When they cleared enough that I could see, a scowl that matched the one on my father's face crept up mine.

Shifters.

Of course, it was shifters.

Out of all the supernaturals they were the ones that I had least sympathy for. The vampires had been cursed. They hadn't asked for eternal life. And the succubi well, they weren't bad per say, they just couldn't seem to help themselves.

The shifters however, wanted to be different - to be the best, the strongest, the fastest. It was why the first shifter hundreds of years ago pleaded to the gods to help them defeat their enemies and conquer all. Too bad they didn't get exactly what they had asked for.

They got faster and stronger alright. But at what price? The moon controlled them until they were strong enough to shift outside of its rays and yet they were easily angered. Even after all this time they were still fighting to see who was the best.

The fucking lot of them needed to be spayed and neutered.

"Sorry we're late." A tall dark-skinned man with an accent that made his words sound more dignified than they should have from a man wearing only ripped up jeans and no shirt. He wore his salt and pepper hair shaved close to his head, his beard long enough to grab on to. Pure white teeth grinned arrogantly in my father's direction. "You see, we had a little change in leadership tonight."

My father, never one to be easily taken by surprise, simply inclined his head. "So, it would seem. Congratulations on your promotion...I don't believe I have met you before..." my father held out a hand toward the new alpha - the leader of the shifters - waiting for him to supply his name.

The six-foot five monster of a man loomed over my father easily and yet he wasn't built in an unpleasant manner. Most were either too lanky for their height or too bulky. This new alpha seemed to have prayed to the gods for some kind of favor because every inch of him was perfectly proportionate to his height. Enough so that the majority of the females were having a hard time taking their eyes off of him.

"Joe," the alpha stated firmly, his accent making the ordinary enough name sound exotic. He provided no sir name, and my father didn't ask for one.

"Very well, Joe." My father said, without skipping a beat, "Welcome to my home. Perhaps next time you can use the front door."

Joe threw his head back and laughed. Toothers, it may have seemed like he was laughing at my father's joke. Except my father hadn't been joking. The threat in his voice was only visible to those who were looking for it. I was always looking for it. Joe hadn't missed it either.

When he finished laughing, Joe shifted his bare feet on the shattered glass on the floor not once wincing. "I suppose I was a bit over enthusiastic to go to my first gathering as alpha." His pitch-black gaze slid around the room - calculating, deciphering, and cataloging. There was not a single thing those eyes missed. Until they came to land on me.

Without requesting permission as most of the other supernaturals would have done, Joe stalked across the room and stopped before me. My cousin stiffened at my side, no more comfortable with the attention the new alpha was giving me than I was.

"You, I've heard of you..." Joe's gaze moved over my form. To his credit they didn't linger on my chest for longer than was polite as he assessed me. "So, you're to be my new master..." he smirked over his shoulder at the other shifters. "Doesn't look like much does she?" His comment caused the shifters to chuckle.

My jaw ticked and yet I held myself in check.

Then...he touched me.

The dirty shifter plopped his hand on top of my head and patted me like a child all the while laughing, "Don't worry little girl. I'll give you a hand in keeping these idiots in line."

Before I could think about it, my hand shot out and grabbed him by the balls. Joe's eyes bugged from his skull and the hand on my head dropped as he roared his pain.

The shifters cried out in fury. I trusted the guards to keep them in check while I taught their alpha a lesson.

I moved closer to him, until our faces were inches apart and hissed, "How about you give yourself a hand and never touch me again."

Joe grunted.

"What was that?" I gave his balls a squeeze.

"Y... yes," he croaked, his face pinched in pain.

I paused for a moment about to let him go...

"That's enough, Crysta."

My eyes narrowed at my father's command. Instead of letting Joe go, I gave him another squeeze. "Yes, what?"

Joe swallowed and stared down at me, hatred filling his eyes as he bit out, "Yes, mistress."

I released him and patted his head, a small smile on my lips. "There's a good boy."

The silence in the ballroom was deafening. The only sound was the rapid beating of each person's heart. As if no one even dared to breathe.

Good.

If I didn't start bringing them to heel now, then once my father finally stepped down, I'd have nothing but chaos. Better to have them be wary of me from the start than to form their own ideas later.

"It seems that we missed quite a bit."

I stepped back from Joe at the sound of Xavier's voice. Schooling my face so as not to give away my embarrassment. Xavier and I didn't have a romantic relationship and yet I didn't like him to see the monster that my father had made of me.

Xavier brushed his thumb against the side of his mouth, picking up a stray bit of blood he'd missed and sucked it into his mouth, his piercing blue eyes on me the entire time. "If I get handsy, will I get you to fondle my bits as well?" A few of the vampires chuckled.

Narrowing my gaze, I let the monster within peek out just a tiny bit. "Come over here and find out."

Taken aback by my words, Xavier's eyes widened, his expression going flat. Then in a blink of an eye that carefree expression was back on his face. "I'll take a rain check. I think we've all had enough excitement for one night, don't you agree, Abraham?"

"Agreed."

My father's voice made me flinch. He'd moved much closer to me without my noticing. Joe had gone back to his pack, his eyes lingering on me with a promise of retribution. Everyone else watched on from a safe distance, either from fear of what I might do or what my father would do. My goal now was to make sure it was always the former.

"I believe we have all had quite enough drama for the night," my father grabbed my elbow and squeezed, a warning to keep quiet. "Thank you all for coming to welcome my daughter into her new position. As you can see, we are going to have our hands full."

No one laughed.

The crowd parted as my father ushered me through the ballroom and up the stairs, his hand never wavering from my arm. I forced a polite mask over my face and pretended I didn't want to jerk my arm away from him. Causing a scene now would do no one any good, least of all me.

He did not release me until we arrived safely behind the closed doors of his study then he practically threw me away from him. "What were you thinking?"

I caught myself on my injured hand before I fell to the floor. I tried to hold back the wince, but he noticed.

"And you're injured." He shook his head and huffed. "That's just great. Not only did you insult every single leader down there, but you almost gave away your one weakness. Our weakness." He stalked toward me, until he knelt before me. "Do you think this is a game? Do you know what they would do to you if they knew about this?" He grabbed my injured hand and shook it, his fingers biting into the open cut.

I gasped, my eyes watering. However, I didn't pull away. I wouldn't give him the satisfaction.

"Your life isn't about you anymore, Crysta," he continued, his grip still on my injury. "You are all that I have left, and I will not have you throw everything away for some childish tantrum." He tossed me back my hand and stood, marching toward his desk.

I drew my hand close to my chest and glared up at him. "So I'm just supposed to let him talk down to me? That the new heir is nothing but a weak-willed flower? Would that have given the better impression?"

My father sighed, rubbing his temples as he sat down. "No, that is not what I mean either. However, you could have handled the situation in a different manner. Shifters are temperamental at best. They only understand strength."

"And did I not show my strength just now?" I made a show of picking myself up off the ground, brushing my gown off and taking a seat across from him as if we were chatting over tea.

He laced his fingers before him and stared at me. "What you did was insult his manhood. You could have beat him down. Hell, shoot him for all I care. But no, you had to choose the one way that would ensure the new alpha hated you."

I snorted. "That was going to happen either way."

"Yes, but now he will seek revenge for making him look weak in front of his pack." My father shifted in his seat, pulling a package of papers out. "Tonight, was just a formality. We will begin your instruction as of tomorrow. You will also go to each house and present yourself, apologize, flatter them, whatever you need to do to smooth things over." He shot me a warning look. "And whatever you do, don't get injured again. We were lucky tonight that no one noticed but we can't count on luck again."

I held my injured hand tightly in my other.

"Now go get that taken care of and go to bed. I'll see you bright and early."

I was dismissed. "Good night, father."

My movements were stiff as I stalked through the hallways. I kept moving until I reached my bedroom. I ripped at the laces of my dress, pulling at it until it was nothing but a heap of fabric on the floor. Wearing nothing but my undergarments, I made for the bathroom.

The water from the tap burned over the cut in my hand, a welcome distraction from the rage in my chest. I waited until the water had cleared most of the dried blood away before searching out the pieces of glass still lodged in my flesh. I cursed when my fingers kept slipping away from them.

"Here, let me."

I sighed and turned to Ines standing in the doorway of my bathroom. "Thanks."

She took my outstretched hand as I sat on the toilet seat. "Tweezers?"

I gestured up toward the cabinet and waited while she retrieved them.

"How you manage to hide such injuries, I'll never know," Ines began while prodding at my hand. "Even though I heal right away it still hurts like a bitch."

I shrugged. "I'm used to it."

"Still," she stared up at me from the tiled floor, pushing her braids over her shoulder as she worked, "you have more resolve than I do. Plus, what you did to that new alpha jerk?" She giggled and shook her head. "That was the highlight of the year. They won't forget you, that's for sure."

I leaned on my other hand and grumbled, "Yeah, that's what Abraham is worried about."

Ines picked out the pieces of glass one at a time, her brows furrowed over her work. "Well, I for one thought it was great. He shouldn't have tried to overstep like that. It'll make them think twice next time."

I grunted while she worked, shaking my hand out when she finished. "Thanks." Ines stood and backed out of the way for me to get to the sink. My face pinched as I rinsed my hand, the stinging more now that Ines had been picking at it.

"So, what are you going to do?"

Patting my hand with a towel, I cocked my head at Ines. "What do you mean?"

"You're not going back to school, right?"

I shook my head. "No. I don't suppose I am." I stared off to the side thinking about how I would explain my withdrawal to Bethany. There was no way she was going to accept some half assed answer. I'd be lucky if she didn't show up out of the blue to drag me back home.

Home. I guess that was here now. For a long time, I had tried to make a home anywhere else but here. In this cold and unfeeling mansion that only cared about power.

"And your brother?"

I jerked my gaze back to Ines. There was a glimmer of hope in her face. As if she were almost afraid to let it flourish. I closed the distance between us and grasped her hands in mine.

"Abraham wants me to go around to the houses and kiss ass because of tonight." I smirked, thinking about how pissed he would be to find out my real plans. "But what better way to find out what they really know about Michael's disappearance?"

CHAPTER 6

WHEN I HAD ONLY just closed my eyes to sleep, my phone beeped with an incoming message. Thinking it was Bethany checking up on me, I turned over and reached for it.

It wasn't Bethany. It was an unknown number with only two words.

Come over.

I didn't have to guess who would demand such a thing from me at this hour. Only one person had the gall to send me a command without stating who they were.

Without responding back, I collapsed back on the bed, my hand over my eyes, the phone still in my hand. I shouldn't go. My father wants to meet bright and early. I don't have time to play around.

Even with all the reasons I shouldn't go whirling through my head, I crawled out of bed and walked to my wardrobe. I withdrew a pair of pants and a blouse pulling them on without bothering to see what I'd grabbed. They'd just get taken off anyway. He'd seen me in worse.

Instead of going for the front door, I went to my balcony. Fifty-nine years old and I still had to sneak out of my room. Would I still be climbing out the balcony window when I was head of the Van Helsing house? I didn't want to think about that right now.

I dropped silently to the ground below. The cobblestone path laid spread out before me without a single obstacle in my way. I didn't bother trying to sneak, having memorized the guard duty years ago. None of them would stop me in any case. Though, they may tell my father.

Let them.

Soon I'd be the one in control and there wasn't anything my father could do about it.

I moved past the shattered ballroom windows, already replaced with temporary glass. Pausing by the windows, I peered inside. The floors had been cleaned and all the glass cleared away as well. The insides were empty and dark; it was as if the events of tonight had never happened.

I glanced down at my bound hand. No it had happened. The pain in my hand proved that as much. A sound from the other end of the path alerted me of someone coming.

I shouldn't doddle here.

My boots crunched the leaves beneath my feet as I crossed the lawn and made for the garage. The lights were still on as I slipped inside the back door.

Lucas sat at a table inside the garage with a few of the other employees. When I walked in he glanced up and smiled. "Feeling a bit restless tonight, miss?"

I smiled in return and walked over to the wall of keys. "I guess you could say that." I grabbed the set I was looking for off the wall and curled my fingers around them. "Figured I could use a bit of fresh air."

The old man inclined his head and turned back to his cards. "Don't stay out too late."

"I won't," I told him ,striding across the garage to the dark red sports bike parked by the family car. Throwing my leg over the bike, I slid the key into the ignition and reached for my helmet. Before pulling it over my head, I said over my shoulder, "Have a good night."

Lucas waved to me while the others watched curiously but didn't question me.

The garage door opened with a click of a button and I covered my face with my helmet, closing the face screen tight. I let the roar of the engine combined with the wind blow away my thoughts. The road wound before me taking me left and right. Like the tug of war going on in my heart.

I said nothing to my father or to Ines and the others. However, it made something inside of me ache to leave the human life I had made behind. To leave my classes. My goal to become a doctor was increasingly becoming nonexistent. Even the cat cafe. I would miss Ryan and the over priced drinks. Most of all...I would miss Bethany. The first human I had ever called a true friend. It would destroy something in me to leave her behind. To never contact her again. And yet I know it's for the best. If I'm to be the heir then Bethany has to stay as far away from me as possible.

Or else...

I rolled over in bed and threw my legs over the side, letting them hang there. As I reached for my pants, the mattress dipped behind me and a large hand wrapped around the back of my neck in a gentle but firm hold.

"Where are you going, my little Van Helsing?" Xavier pressed his mouth to the side of my neck in a series of hot wet kisses, letting his fangs tease along my pulse. He made my family name sound like a dirty word. To the supernaturals in the world, it probably was.

"Don't call me that. I have to get home before anyone misses me." I shrugged off his hand and his kisses, searching Xavier's disheveled room for my panties. Finding the pink lace hanging off a lamp, I stood to grab them.

Hands dropped to my waist and in one swift movement jerked me back onto bed. "But I would miss you, pet. Isn't that enough?"

I twisted in Xavier's embrace, my eyes drifting down the long expansion of his pale hairless chest before lingering on the criss cross shaped scars. He must have gotten them pre-death for them to linger after.

Lifting my gaze to his stunningly blue eyes that would leave a nun weeping, I leaned in close and clipped, "No."

When I tried to stand once more, Xavier's hands drifted south until they found my naked flesh still sensitive from our latest activities.

"Stop it," I breathed. My words said one thing and yet I did not push his circling fingers away. Two digits pressed inside of me and my head fell back against his waiting chest.

I allowed myself a moment of weakness, giving into the pleasure of his touch. Xavier's free hand cupped my left breast, his cock hard and ready against my back. I wiggled against it, my will to fight back quickly dwindling.

After all...who would miss me? My father didn't expect me until morning and that was still hours away.

"Oh," Xavier murmured against my ear as he made me coo with need. "You were magnificent tonight. So deadly beautiful. A rose just riddled with thorns."

I bucked against his hand, demanding him to shut up and give me what I wanted already.

"Everyone wanted you. I could smell it." He sucked in a deep breath, breathing in my scent and groaning. "Everyone wants a piece of little Crysta Van Helsing." His fingers flexed inside of me. I cried out, squeezing my eyes shut tight. "I wonder...what would old Abraham think of his precious heir writhing in the arms of the enemy? So wet..." he scratched his fangs along my throat and my insides clenched around his fingers tight, "...such a needy little blood whore."

My eyes snapped open and in a flash I was out of the bed, my Colt pointed at his chest as he laughed.

"What is it, my little Van Helsing? Have I struck a nerve?" Xavier lifted his hand still coated in my juices and licked each digit in slow procession, his eyes locking with mine.

"You're disgusting. This," I gestured between the two of us with my gun, "means nothing. You are nothing to me," I bit the words out between tight lips, my finger aching to pull the trigger on his beautiful laughing face.

Xavier pouted and sat up further. "Could you really kill me, pet? Put a bullet straight through my undead heart?" He placed his hands over his chest, his eyes watching me with curious intent.

He didn't think I'd do it. Of course he didn't. It wasn't the first time I'd threatened him. So it was no surprise he didn't take me seriously.

I let my mind go blank and my eyes narrow, releasing the safety on my Colt. My voice was steady and cold when I answered, "Yes."

For the first time, that playful smile of his dropped. His brows drew together tight as he lowered his arms to hang over his knees. "You would really do it, wouldn't you?"

My expression never wavered. "It's what I do."

Cursing in Romanian, Xavier shook his head and chuckled. The master vampire slipped out of the bed, not caring about his nakedness as he stalked toward me. He didn't stop until the barrel of my gun was pressed right up against his lower chest. Too low to hit his heart but it would hurt just the same.

"Don't push me, Xavier."

Xavier grabbed the barrel of my gun and shifted it up to point at his heart. "What's worse? A monster who knows what he is or one that pretends to be otherwise?"

He didn't wait for me to answer his odd question.

"You Van Helsings have a god complex like no other and forget you're just as bad as the rest of us." Xavier pushed against the barrel until it had to be biting into his flesh, while he whispered harshly, "There's a reason you're the ones the monsters are afraid of."

Expression unchanged, I squeezed the trigger. The click resounded in the room and a satisfying feeling came over me as Xavier's eyes widened, then narrowed as he realized I'd been bluffing once more. The Colt wasn't even loaded.

I put the pistol back into my holster and slipped the rest of my clothing back on. With the holster pressed against either side of my breasts, I felt whole again. "One of these days, it won't be empty Xavier. Remember that."

The vampire's fangs flashed at me as he mockingly tipped an imaginary hat at me. "I pray that day never comes, Mistress Van Helsing."

I snorted at the honorific before turning my back on him. I didn't bother closing the door behind me, leaving him naked to anyone who passed by. Not that anyone would. The place was deserted. One of many of Xavier's properties. The only ones who knew about it were a select few and unlike some of the other supernaturals, Xavier kept such a tight leash on them that they wouldn't dare to act as if they knew anything of our affairs.

Halfway down the stairs and Xavier called after me. I paused and turned. He leaned against the railing, completely at ease in his nudity.

"What do you want?" I let my irritation color my words.

Xavier ignored my tone and cocked his head to the side to ask, "What are you going to do about Michael?"

I frowned at his question. "You heard my father. There's nothing to be done. Best to focus on the future of the Van Helsing clan."

Xavier laughed, the sound making my chest tight. "Like I'd ever believe you'd give up on your brother without a fight."

Spinning away from him, I stomped down the stairs and bit out, "Believe it or not, I don't care."

"Sure you don't." Xavier's words and laughter chased after me until the doors of the house closed behind me.

I swung a leg over my bike and revved the engine to life. Pulling my hair back before putting on my helmet, I stared hard at the road ahead. I'd spent too much time with Xavier. He was getting to know me a bit too well.

That'd have to change.

I couldn't have anyone knowing what I planned. Not even him.

My father might not give a rat's ass about Michael, however, I wasn't going to leave him to rot. Not again. This Van Helsing will come home, even if it's just to have a body to bury.

CHAPTER 7

THE SUN WAS COMING up over the horizon by the time I arrived back at the mansion. I'd spent the last few hours just driving around.

Xavier had given me a lot to think about.

Was I just like my father? Was I just another monster hiding behind the name of protecting the ignorant humans? Or was this just another one of Xavier's mind games to make me question myself and not take it out on him?

The garage door stood open for me before I even pulled up to the front. My cousin, Eric was waiting with his hands in his pockets looking very much the douche canoe he was.

The thought made me think of Bethany. She'd been the one to teach me some of the newer creative slang this generation was using. Douche canoe was one of her favorites.

I needed to message her soon.

"There's the runaway princess." Eric grinned at me squinting into the morning light. "We were just about to send a search party out for you."

I parked my bike and pulled off my helmet. "You could have just called me."

"We did," Eric countered, following me as I stalked toward the kitchen door. "You didn't answer."

I reached for my phone, usually tucked into my back pocket and found it empty.

Fuck. Of course.

"I've seemed to have misplaced it," I grumbled as I entered the kitchen. "My apologies for the hassle."

When I entered the kitchen, a shriek hit my ears before I was enveloped into a warm doughy embrace. Realizing it was Ana, I relaxed and patted her on the back.

"Why such the welcome?" I asked, pulling slightly away.

Ana jerked back and smacked me on top of the head. I winced. "Don't you dare do that again! Do you know how worried we've been?" Her face grew red and blotchy before crumbling into tears. "After we just lost your brother? I don't think my heart can handle losing another one."

Guilt ripped at my insides and I reached for Ana. She waved me away, swiping at her eyes as she shifted around. "No. No. Don't hug me. I'll just cry more." Then she shot me a warning look. "Next time answer your phone."

I offered up a contrite smile. "I will as soon as I find it."

Ana shook her head. "Young people nowadays. Never keeping up with your things. You'd think you'd know where it is since it's permanently attached to your hand."

I giggled and patted her on the shoulders. "Of course, Ana. You're right. I'll get right on that."

"First," Eric said, reminding me of his presence, "You should go see your father."

I glared over my shoulder at the suggestion.

Eric locked his gaze with mine not wilting under the weight of my glare. Then after a couple of seconds he blinked and scratched the back of his head, a lopsided grin on his face. "I mean, if you don't want to get yelled at."

I snorted. "You mean even more yelled at." I had no illusions that if the rest of the household was in such an uproar about my nighttime trip, my father would be absolutely livid.

Sighing, I shook my head. "Better face the music." I grabbed an apple on my way through the kitchen, Ana calling out after me, "Come back and eat something substantial afterward."

Biting into my apple, I let the sweet juice of it fill my mouth. I best savor this now because knowing my father he wouldn't give me the chance to go back to the kitchens for a while.

"Are you going to follow me the whole way?" I asked Eric once we reached the upstairs hallway.

Eric shrugged sheepishly. "Actually, I wanted to ask you something..."

I stopped and turned to him. "What is it?"

He made a show of shifting and shoving his hands into his pockets and then out again. "Well, you know, last night...how you..."

I huffed. "Eric. Father is waiting for me. Spit it out already."

His face pinched then he blurted. "Did you have a knife in your dress too?"

My brows furrowed together. "What?"

Eric gestured to my bandaged hand. "Your hand. You obviously got cut by a Van Helsing blade or it would have healed right?"

I forced myself not to react and schooled my face, not giving anything away. In a matter-of-fact tone, I said, "Yes. I cut myself on my own knife during the commotion."

Nodding like he had known that already, Eric chuckled, "I was wondering why you were trying to hide it. I'd have been so embarrassed to have cut myself on my own blade. Especially in front of all the houses."

"Right," I bit out with a jerk of my head. "Embarrassed."

I started walking again and then paused turning back to Eric. "Can you not mention this to anyone?" I offered him a sheepish smile. "I'd hate to give off the wrong impression on my first day."

Eric gave me a two-finger salute. "Aye captain. It'll be our little secret."

I beamed at him. "Great. Thanks."

Taking a bite out of my apple, I used it as an excuse not to say anything else. Thankfully, Eric didn't follow me any further.

That was a close one. Too close.

I'd thought I'd gotten away with it but it seems I was too caught up in the alpha drama to notice Eric watching me. Hopefully, he was the only one who noticed and would keep it to himself.

I finished off my apple as I approached father's study. I glanced around for somewhere to put the core and not finding a waste bin sat it down on a nearby table. I'd grab it on the way out or a servant would grab it first.

Steeling myself for a long extensive lecture, I turned the doorknob and entered. Abraham stood before the fireplace staring up at my mother's portrait.

Did he do that a lot? I wouldn't know. The last few days were the most time I've spent with him at once. Usually, it was only to lecture me or tell me what he had planned for me. It almost seemed like he was happy to send me to the human school, so I'd be out of the way.

Closing the door behind me, I waited before his desk to acknowledge me. No use making him start the lecture before he had to.

Unfortunately, I didn't have long to wait.

"There will be no more sneaking out for midnight rendezvous with that vampire lover of yours."

My entire body stiffened.

Had I heard him, right? He knew about Xavier? How? When? We had been so careful...

My father turned slightly to give me a flat look. "Oh, yes, I know of your affair. I've known for quite some time."

I didn't deny it or confirm his words.

"At first, I was disgusted. How could any child of mine allow themselves to be tainted by one of the very creatures we fight against." He stared up at my mother's picture with a look of disgust marring his face. He turned from the painting and moved over to his desk. "Then I thought perhaps it is just a phase. Childish curiosity." He let his lips curl up slightly at the edges. "I would be lying if I were to say I too hadn't dabbled with the beasts just to see what all the fuss was about. And yet, I never once fell in love with one."

I started forward. "I'm not-"

My father held his hand up, cutting me off. "I'm not finished." I clenched my teeth tightly together. "Whether you love Xavier or not makes no difference to me. You will end it and end it now. We cannot have the other houses thinking you are favoring the vampires above the others."

I stared hard at him. Nothing I would say would convince him from what he had already decided himself.

Abraham's eyes locked with mine. "Am I understood?"

"Yes, father," I bit out, my fingers curled tightly into balls at my sides. "Is that all?"

"No." He opened a draw and then tossed something to me. It was a cell phone. "I trust you won't lose this one."

I jerked my head once.

"I took the liberty of having all the phone numbers you will ever need programmed inside." He didn't wait for me to answer before turning his back to me. "Have breakfast and report to training. I'm sure you're sorely behind and we can't have our enemies using your weakness against you."

I hid my injured hand behind me, knowing he wasn't just referring to my physical strength.

"Then be prepared to leave before dinner. We visit Lilith's Touch first. Then the Den of Shadows. Though," He huffed a cruel laugh. "I don't suppose you need a private introduction there."

I bit my lip to keep from lashing out.

"However, it would look out of sorts if we don't have you visit them all." He sighed and shook his head, his gaze up on my mother once more. I waited for him to continue but after a few moments of silence he sat down in his chair and went to work as if I was never in the room to begin with.

Shoving my new phone into my back pocket, I spun on my heel and left. The door closed quietly behind me. Much more quietly than the roar of emotions whipping around inside of me.

My eyes flickered to the side table where the apple core still sat. I snatched it up and stalked to the nearest balcony. I shut the doors behind me and threw the core as far as I could screaming loudly for all to hear.

I yelled until my voice went raspy and the guards had gathered below my perch. Once they saw it was me, they gave each other a curious unsure look before moving back to their positions.

I couldn't even lose control here without having an audience.

Fuck.

A bitter laugh escaped. Apparently, I couldn't even do that without anyone knowing either.

I gripped the side of the balcony letting the cold metal seep into my palms and I sagged forward. I let my breath go in and out until I felt as if my insides weren't going to explode.

Abruptly, I pivoted back inside. Waiting for me by the doorway stood Jerrod. He leaned against the wall with a concerned frown.

"Feel better?"

I nodded once. "Yeah. Now I need to hit something."

"Well, for once I'm glad to say it won't be me." Jerrod laughed, clapping me on the shoulder.

My stomach rumbled. "Food first though."

Jerrod's face went white. "Uh, I'll just meet you in the training room."

I laughed at him. "Ana still hasn't forgiven you, huh?"

Face curling inward, Jerrod crossed his arms over his stomach and hunched. "Hey, don't make fun. I'm going to have to eat out every meal this weekend at this rate."

I shook my head and smirked. "Will teach you not to mess with her food next time, won't it?"

"Yeah, but I heard she gave you a good wallop this morning," Jerrod slid a sly look in my direction.

Wincing, I rubbed my head where she'd hit me. "Yeah, well, I guess I deserved it. I forgot that I was the precious heir now and can't just go off the grid like that."

"Yep," Jerrod lifted his arms over his head and stretched. "Life of the rich and famous."

I grunted. "Who in their right mind would want that?"

CHAPTER 8

GROANING AS I STRETCHED my left arm up and over my head, I leaned off the opposite side lengthening out my side. A satisfying ache pulled at my side as I reached even further to the right. Jerrod and the others really put me through my paces today.

Did my father tell them to kick my ass or was I really that out of practice? Either way, I needed to get back in shape. Who knew what I was going to be up against now that I was the official heir?

I frowned and paused before my bedroom door.

The heir. A title I never wanted or expected to have. And yet, here I was with the position anyone else in the Van Helsing clan would kill to have.

I blew out a hard breath and shook my head. If only they knew the bull shit that came with being the child of the head. I'd trade places with just about any of them right now.

About as much as I longed for a warm bath to soothe my aching muscles before I had to put on my mask tonight. I scowled at my door, crossing my arms under my chest. Tonight. Tonight, I would have to smooth things over with the succubi.

Though Azeryth was the one who had started it, I'd acted rashly. I could have defused the situation with more political tact than pulling out my weapon. A weak person relies on violence to defend themselves against conflict. I was not a weak person. Short tempered, but not weak. I'd have to work on that now that I would be forced to interact more with the other supernatural houses.

"Crysta!"

I jerked, dropping my arms as I slowly turned toward the panicked Eric running toward me. "What is it?"

Eric stopped before me and bent at the waist, his hands on his knees as he caught his breath. "You need...to...to...come quick." He held a hand up and swallowed another breath. "Sorry," he chuckled slightly, "Need more cardio...damn..."

I cocked my head to the side and simply waited. He'd tell me when he was ready. Any additional comments would only deter him into a conversation I didn't want to have. I glanced longingly at my bedroom door, expecting I wasn't going to get that bath I wanted after all.

Finally, Eric stood up and swiped his forehead and shook his head. "Man, those stairs are killer on the glutes."

I offered a polite smile, still waiting for what he had stopped me for. Get on with it already.

"Sorry, you must just be thinking shut up and tell me already huh?" A sheepish grin crept up Eric's face.

I stayed silent. No need to point it out since he had.

"Anyway..." he continued, clucking his tongue. "You better get down to the rec room. There's been a development."

I cocked a brow. "What kind of development?" Nothing important ever happened in the rec room. It was a place we Van Helsings went to hang out and unwind. You could watch television. Play games. Or just sit around and do nothing, though anyone caught doing that would for sure get extra duties.

Eric's expression darkened as if he didn't want to tell me. He came here to get me. So, it must be something to do with me. Why else would he have come?

My patience wearing thin, I sighed and rubbed my forehead. "Eric, I have to get ready for tonight. I don't mean to be rude, but could you just tell me? I won't kill the messenger I promise."

"I know, I know..." Eric huffed a laugh and waved me off. "Of all the people to be chosen as the next heir, I'm glad it's you. Your brother was just -" he cut himself off and shot a look to the side grimacing. "Sorry, there I go running my mouth off."

"It's fine." I gritted my teeth together, my patience at its end.

"Anyway, Ines needs you." Eric pointed back down the hallway. "She got a package in the mail and then just went into hysterics. She won't let anyone see it but you. So could you..."

I didn't let him finish, shoving past him and running down the hallway. My heart pounded in my ears as I raced down the stairs. Ines wasn't one to go into hysterics. She was one of the most put together people that I knew. She could be facing down death itself and still not quiver or shed a tear.

However...there was one person...one singular person who could cause all logic to go out the window.

Michael.

My brother was her day and night. Her very reason for being. Some might call her love for him weakness and it still might be. It also gave her an overwhelming strength. A reason for being above her own life. Because as obsessed Ines was with Michael, he was equally enamored by her.

Love like that...would I ever experience it? In my sixty years of life, I'd never loved anyone the way that Ines loved my brother. If I hadn't witnessed their love in person, I might never believe such a thing existed. The gods knew, my father certainly wasn't the shiny example of caring and compassion.

So, the only people I could look to were my brother and Ines. I would do everything in my power to make sure that love survived. Even after the grave.

I heard the commotion before I entered the rec room. The voices overlapped one another so much that I couldn't understand anything anyone was saying. I certainly couldn't hear Ines.

Once I stepped into the room, I searched for Ines's dark braided head of hair. Unfortunately, there were too many people in the way to get a lock on her. However, they were all congregated around one area. The area that I could safely assume held Ines at the center.

Jerrod saw me before I saw him, shouting out my name and waving me down. As I stalked toward them the crowd parted and the expressions were a mix of emotions, I hadn't expected.

Pity.

Disgust.

Horror.

Shame.

On and on it went across each face and into the sea of Van Helsings. Not a single person was happy about what was at the center of the room.

I tried to brace myself for what was to come but nothing could brace me for what awaited me. Not the utter agony on Ines's face nor the small package in her hand.

When her brown eyes met mine, my steps faltered. My heart stuttered in my chest, and I had to swallow down a large lump in my throat.

"Crysta," Ines's eyes watered, and she turned her face away from me or the box, I wasn't sure which until I got closer.

My gaze fell on the box, and I frowned. I couldn't figure out what it was that I was looking at. When my mind finally caught up with my eyes, it took everything I had not to vomit there on the spot.

An eyeball with the cord still attached stared blindly up from a small red box. It took me a moment to realize that the green and gold eye was one that I recognized. Bile billowed up in my throat.

"Crysta?" Anyone else would think Jerrod was asking me if I was alright. I knew he was reminding me to keep it together in front of half of our clan and especially for Ines. I could freak out later. I had to be the heir now.

I knelt before Ines and reached for the box. She clutched it in her hands, those same hands trembling with fear. "Ines," I murmured, looking at her and not the eye in the box. "It's alright. You can let me have it."

With shaking hands Ines held the box out to me, her eyes staring off to the side at nothing. I grasped the box with both hands, trying my best not to look at the eye for too long. Jerrod handed me the lid to the box. I took my time putting it on before standing.

"Did anyone see anything?" I turned away from Ines, holding the box carefully in my hands. "Who delivered it? Anything?"

Jerrod shook his head. "No. No one saw anything -"

"It was...it was...in my room."

Brows raised, I spun around to Ines. "In your room?"

She jerked her head once, her hands clenched tightly into fists at her sides.

I hummed. "So, not only were they able to get on the property but get inside." I glanced down at the box in my hands. "How did they know which room was yours?"

Jerrod shrugged. "Had to be someone who knows the mansion. You don't think it's one of us, do you?"

I hated to think about it but there was no other explanation. Someone had gone so far as to put it in Ines's room. They wanted her to find it. And to send her a piece of Michael's body? What did it mean? Was there a significance in sending the eye? Like they were watching?

Turning my attention back to Jerrod, I shook my head. "We can't know that until further investigation. Have someone check the video surveillance. With any luck they didn't know how to avoid them."

"And if they did?" Jerrod cocked his head to the side.

"Then it's more likely to be someone from the inside." I paused and shot a look over my shoulder toward the loitering Van Helsings in the hallway. "Someone knows where Michael is and if he's alive. We'll start questioning everyone and see what they -"

"Crysta."

I stopped. "Don't worry, Ines. We'll figure this out. I promise."

Without warning she grabbed my wrist, jerking me to her. Those horror filled eyes were now full of desperation. "He's alive."

My brows furrowed together. "What do you mean he's alive?"

She shoved a crinkled piece of paper in my hand before pulling back from me. I carefully opened it so as not to damage it further and scanned its contents.

The handwriting wasn't something I recognized but it was easy to see why Ines thought Michael was still alive.

How many pieces can a Van Helsing lose before they finally die?

Let's find out.

My teeth gnashed together so hard that my jaw ached.

"What is it?" Jerrod asked, stepping to me. I showed him the note. "She didn't show us this. Ines came barreling in here a bit ago with that box without saying anything. I was lucky to get anything out of her to know to send for you."

"It's alright," I said more for Ines's benefit than Jerrod's. "We know now." I held the box with one hand and placed the other on my hip and sighed. "On the positive side, we have confirmation that Michael is alive."

Ines scoffed. "You find that positive?" she jerked her hand toward the box. "They're mutilating him! How is that in any way positive?"

I placed my hand on her shoulder and leaned down to her. "Because that means he'll come back to us. Even if he's missing a piece or two."

Ines visibly swallowed her eyes watering as she nodded.

"That also means we have a time limit on finding him," Jerrod reminded us with the note.

I grimaced. That was going to be a problem. We didn't know how often they were going to send pieces of Michael - and there was little doubt that they wouldn't send another one - or how long we had. Why now? Had they been holding him this entire time? Why start now? There was no ransom, no threat to kill him if we didn't comply with their wishes. What did they want?

"Should we tell your father?" Jerrod added on shifting in place. His discomfort on the topic was obvious. He was closer to me than to Michael but still none of us wanted to think about one of our own being tortured in such a way.

I huffed. "If we don't, someone else will. They all saw the box. Someone will mention it to him and it's best if we are the first."

"What about the note?" Ines muttered, wrapping her arms around herself. "Will you tell him about it?"

"I'm not sure. I probably should." My lips twisted to one side. "Though, I'm not sure how much good it would do. To him, Michael is as good as dead."

I held the note in my hand and thought carefully about my next steps. They were toying with us. It was all a game to them, whoever they were. A game I was fully prepared to play and win.

CHAPTER 9

"WHAT DO YOU EXPECT me to do about this?" Abraham's tone was just this side of boredom. As if we were talking about the weather and not the possibility of his own son being alive.

I gritted my teeth and slammed my hands on the top of his desk, making the box with Michael's eye bounce. "I expect you to act like a father and worry for your son."

"You think I don't?" he arched his brow, his hands laced before him. "I cannot just think about my own personal feelings in this matter. I have to think of the clan as a whole."

"This is for the good of the clan." I couldn't hold back my temper any longer, my words coming out as a shout. "Michael is part of this clan!"

My father blinked. "Until yesterday your brother was alive and well to everyone but those who are a part of the House of Van Helsing. Have you not stopped to think about why they have sent this now? Right after I announced you as my new heir and Michael as dead?"

I pursed my lips together tightly. "I don't know."

He reached across the desk and tapped the top of the box. "Even if this truly belonged to Michael, which I highly doubt, why would they conveniently wait until I told the rest of the supernatural community to let it be known that he was still alive?"

"To throw us off our game?" I offered up, not liking where this conversation was going.

My father nodded, lifting his hands before him. "We cannot afford to show any sign of weakness while we are in this fragile time. You have only just become the heir. We must show a strong united front to the rest of the supernatural community, or they will devour us."

"And what of Michael? Do we just do nothing?"

He let out a slow breath and turned toward the picture of mother. "As much as I wish your brother was still alive, I have been disappointed too many times to get my hopes up now. Until we have further proof of life, we will not focus our efforts on retrieving him."

I held back my need to call him a heartless asshole. If there was one thing I knew about my father without question, it was that once he had his mind set on something he didn't change it. I could harp at him until the end of time and he would still stand firm.

"Anything else?"

"No."

"Good, then prepare for this evening's festivities." He waved a hand over his shoulder. "We will be dining at Lilith's Touch so dress accordingly."

"Very well." I inclined my head.

"And Crysta," he added before I could move, "Don't start any fights this time."

I glared at the back of his chair and grabbed the box from the table before pivoting on my heel.

"And before I forget..."

I resisted the urge to scream at him, pausing and waiting for him to continue.

"Please send my regards to Ines. I know how trying this must have been for her."

My fingers twitched to pull my Colt out and shoot holes into the back of Abraham's chair until the floor ran red with his blood. Instead, I gave a curt nod and stalked from the room. I kept the door from slamming just barely before stomping down the hallway. I kept moving until I reached my bedroom and shut the door behind me.

I sat the box on my desk and took a deep breath. Letting it out, I slammed my fist against the wall over and over again until the plaster broke and my hand stung from the pain. Blood poured from the cuts on my knuckles but I couldn't bring myself to care.

Why was I surprised by my father's decision? Didn't I know him better than that by now? He would never show weakness because of one of us. If it really came down to it, he would always choose the future of the whole clan over any individual. In his eyes, we were all expendable.

"Fine," I muttered to myself, pulling my hand in front of me so I could survey the damage I had done. "If he won't do what is needed to preserve this family, then I will." I curled my fingers into a fist and winced. That was easier said than done.

Jerrod was looking into the surveillance while Ines was checking her room for any forced entry. If we were lucky then we'd find something to lead us to Michael's captors. If not, then all we could do was wait for another piece to drop into our laps. Literally.

Dragging a hand over my face, I walked across my room and into the bathroom. Turning on the tap, I rinsed my hand off, gritting my teeth with each sting of water on the cuts. I'd have to wear gloves tonight or be questioned for the injuries.

Why did my father have to fall for a human of all people? It seems like it has done nothing but give him heartache and pain. Not to forget, the constant threat hanging over my own head. I couldn't even imagine what would happen if the supernatural community found out the weak link they had been searching for all this time was me.

I snorted. As if my life had that much meaning. Sixty years playing human and hunter has taught me one thing. No one was special. We all had our faults and our strengths. And we all die just the same. Alone.

Having friends or lovers only added onto what your enemies could use against you. At least, that's how my father felt and from what I could tell most of the other Van Helsings. Bethany had taught me differently. Friends could be great assets. They would be there for you even when you weren't there for yourself. They pulled you up when you were down. And a true friend would have your back even when you weren't there to protect it.

That reminded me.

I pulled my new cell phone out of my pocket and swiped open the messaging app. I stopped. I forgot I didn't have any of my usual phone numbers in this phone. That included Bethany's.

Ugh. I slapped my forehead with my free hand, wincing when I realized it was my injured hand. I hadn't talked to Bethany since yesterday morning. My phone was probably blowing up with missed calls and messages from her. I hated to make her worry, but I didn't have any way to get her number just now. If only, I hadn't lost my phone.

I wondered where I'd lost it anyway. I'd had it before I left to meet up with Xavier... my eyes narrowed. That damn vampire. He must have stolen it when I wasn't paying attention. Why though? There wasn't anything on it that could give away our secrets. What was he playing at?

Scowling, I sat my phone aside. No use worrying about it right now. I needed to get through tonight and then I could get a hold of Gerald and see if he could get Bethany my new number while he was picking up my things.

In any case, I had to focus on tonight. There was enough going on without me having to worry about my human life causing me drama.

I finished cleaning up my hand and walked back into my room. Going over to my wardrobe, I pulled open the doors and pursed my lips. To my relief, my father hadn't left me something to wear for tonight. I wouldn't have worn it anyway.

Last night was a formal event. Tonight, I would be meeting the succubi face on with the full force of my position behind me. It wasn't just some event to show me off. I'll be expected to show what kind of leader I will be. I had to make an impression, one that tells them who I was not who my father wanted me to be. Regardless of if I planned on saving Michael and letting him take his rightful place as the heir.

I curled my fingers into a fist and gritted my teeth. The gruesome image of Michael's eye was embedded into my brain, I could see it even now. I closed my eyes and sighed. We had to figure this out and get him back before they started hacking on important parts of him.

Some would say I was being optimistic thinking Michael was still alive. I wasn't. I could feel it in my gut. Michael was out there. I just had to find him.

Removing my current pants, I slid a pair of worn brown leather up my legs. No dresses today. No weapons hidden beneath my skirts. I would be showing my aggression for all to see. A forest green sleeveless shirt followed. Wrapping a cream-colored corset with little red and green flowers around my waist, I pulled the straps up and over my shoulders. My fingers deftly laced up the red laces and pulled it tight. Corsets were never my thing. A tiny waist? Who needed it? However, I couldn't just wear a bullet proof vest all the time. The corset gave my fragile organs much needed protection from any stray attacks as well as not letting on that I needed the protection in the first place.

I let out a long breath. It was so complicated being me.

A knock sounded on my door as I stepped up to my desk. I glanced over to the door while pulling on my gun holster. "Come in."

Ines inched the door open, her eyes down on the ground.

That didn't bode well.

I frowned and stepped toward her. "Is everything alright?"

Ines shook her head and balled her fingers into fists. "I couldn't find anything. Not. A. Damn. Thing." Her whole body wobbled with rage. She jerked her face up and glowered. Not mad at me but at herself. "This whole time he's been alive and I didn't do anything. Nothing. I can't even catch the coward who sent me the package. How can I be worthy of his love?"

I scowled and crossed my arms. "If that's not the stupidest thing I've ever heard."

"See," she stepped forward and raised a fist, "you agree with me. How can I possibly be worthy of marrying the heir of the Van Helsing clan if I can't even track down his captor?"

Huffing, I stalked over to her and smacked her over the head. "No, I mean, it's stupid that you think you have to be worthy of someone's love."

"Hey, don't hit me," she whined. Ines grabbed her head and rubbed it.

"Your abilities don't dictate whether or not you are worthy of being loved. It's about what someone else sees inside of you that matters."

Ines turned her head away. "I don't know what he even sees in me."

I smirked, scratching the side of my face. "Well, you got me there."

"Hey!" Ines growled, glaring at me for real. "You're supposed to be comforting me, not making fun of me."

I cocked my head to the side. "But you're not crying now, are you?"

Ines paused. "Uh...yeah. I guess not."

"Anyway," I waved her off. "I didn't really expect you to find anything. If they've been hidden this long, I doubt they would trip up now and let us catch them."

"Yes, I suppose you're right." Ines sucked in a hard breath before releasing it. "It's still frustrating though."

I nodded. "Yep. Let's just hope that Jerrod had more luck on his side." A large figure appeared in my doorway. "Speak of the devil."

Jerrod's lips quirked up. "Talking about me?" He scuffed his nose with his thumb. "Well, I can't help it if my reputation precedes me."

Ines clucked her tongue. "No one was talking about you. Your head's big enough already."

"Hey now," Jerrod grasped his chest. "Be nice to me or I won't tell you what I found."

That comment made Ines and me straighten up quickly.

Ines grabbed Jerrod by the collar and lifted him into the air, shaking him slightly. "What did you find? Tell me. Right now."

I flinched. Jerrod should know better than to dangle something like that over Ines's head. That's a good way to get killed.

Jerrod held his hands up and chuckled sheepishly. "Alright, alright. Just put me down already. It's bad enough when Crysta kicks my ass. I don't need the others to see me being manhandled by you."

I snorted. "Would serve you right."

Ines dropped him and stepped back. "Don't make me regret not kicking your ass here and now. Tell me. What. Did. You. Find?"

"You better stop delaying," I warned him. "I won't stop her if she decides to kill you."

"I won't kill him," Ines smirked. "Just maim him a little bit."

"Oh, geez. Calm down already. I was just trying to have a little fun. You know lighten up the mood some. Don't gotta go losing your head. Or mine for that matter." Jerrod pulled his phone out of his pocket and pushed a few things on the screen before holding it up for Ines and me to see.

A video of the back of the mansion security camera appeared. At first there was nothing there, just the guards changing shifts. Then I almost missed it. A figure jumped down from an upper level and then darted out of the frame.

"Wait a second," Ines reached for the phone. Jerrod pulled it back before she could get a hand on it. "Hey, let me see that."

Jerrod shook his head, taking a step back and holding it up high above Ines's head. "And have you break it? No way."

Knowing how right Jerrod was, I stepped up behind Ines and placed my hand on her arm. "He's right. If you break his phone, then we can't see who it was. Just take a moment."

Ines shot a look of hatred in my direction then ground her teeth together. She closed her eyes and tensed, breathing in and out several times before opening her eyes once more. "Fine. I'm good." Jerrod arched his brow. "I mean it, I'm fine. Just show us again."

Jerrod's gaze slid over to me briefly.

I jerked my head once.

He lowered the phone once more and pressed a part of the screen. The video replayed except this time Jerrod stopped it just as the figure appeared. "There." Jerrod pointed out at the lower right corner of the screen. "That's right before you found the box right, Ines?"

Ines squinted at the screen and pursed her lips. "Yes, just about. But who is that?"

Jerrod shrugged. "No clue."

"Crysta?" Ines turned to me. "Do you recognize them?"

I reached out for the phone and Jerrod tensed. I gave him a stern look before he handed it over to me. Lifting the phone up to my face, I searched the figure for any sign of familiarity.

My eyes widened.

That ink creeping up each arm, that floppy hair, and I'd never forget that self-satisfied smirk. Once was enough to have it imprinted in my brain. I was disappointed I hadn't noticed the swagger in that athletic build the first time around.

"You've thought of something, haven't you?" Ines closed the space between us, standing at my side.

I inclined my head and turned to her. "Don't you?"

Ines looked closer at the screen as well. "Wait...isn't that?"

"Yep." I handed the phone back to Jerrod. "That's the succubi's very own prince, Azeryth."

Jerrod stared down at the screen, frowning. "You can tell that?"

I snorted. "You need to get your eyes checked." I cracked my knuckles and smirked. "I guess it's a good thing that we're going to Lilith's Touch first. It'll give me just the excuse to question our suspicious prince and finally get some answers."

CHAPTER 10

A BLACK LIMO WAITED in front of the mansion. My father couldn't do anything half assed. He just had to put a show on whenever he left the house which he rarely did for anything other than formal meetings. If I had it my way, I would get rid of the whole damn ritual.

Why couldn't the supernaturals get with the times? Send an email. A text message. Rather than parading ourselves before them like we're the rulers surveying their homes and culture. Policing the supernatural was not the same thing as ruling them. No matter how much my father wished otherwise.

Gerald stood by the limo. His usual shades were discarded for the evening light. He opened the door to the limo for me as I approached.

I nodded my thanks but stopped just inside the door, making my father wait inside. "Have you gone by the school yet to get my things?"

Gerald's gaze met mine, his face unreadable. "Not as of yet. I will go tomorrow if you wish."

"Yes, I would appreciate it." I paused and glanced toward the darkness in the limo before leaning toward Gerald and lowering my voice. "Could you pass on my contact information to Bethany as well?"

Gerald's lips quirked up at the edges and he inclined his head. "Of course."

I bobbed my head in thanks and slid into the limo. As Gerald closed the door behind me, my father spoke, not turning away from the papers in his lap, "Finally. You will need to demolish that habit of yours."

I scowled. "What habit?"

"Speaking to the help as if they were your friends and not here to serve you." He glanced up from his papers to give me a stern look. "You are the Van Helsing heir and should act as such."

I resisted the urge to roll my eyes and met Lucas's gaze through the rearview mirror and muttered, "Perhaps, that is something we should change."

My father didn't bother to respond though I knew he heard me. It was fine by me. I was still upset with him about his reaction to Michael being alive. The less I had to speak to him the better. There were other things to keep me occupied on the way to the succubi's lair.

Lilith's Touch.

In all my sixty years, I'd never been to the establishment myself. However, I knew many Van Helsings including my brothers who frequented the club almost as much as they were at home. While Lilith's Touch was the home of all the succubi in the area, it was first and foremost a strip club.

It was quite ingenious really. A species of demons who fed on sexual energy running an establishment known for causing exactly that. They had an endless supply of food and were paid for it. The humans were none the wiser. In fact, the succubi are one of the only supernaturals with a power that had the potential to completely incapacitate a Van Helsing.

While the Van Helsings could not be killed by any weapon not created by their own, that rule did not apply to our energy. They could feed on our energy until they were full to the brim and still, we would not die. At least, that was the assumption. I'd never seen the act put to use so I couldn't say for sure if we did have an end to our energy or if it would continue to rebuild itself as it was drained.

The same could be said for Michael and his captor. Would he die with each part removed? Or would he end up being just a pile of parts, his consciousness there forever screaming for death.

We pulled up to the front of Lilith's Touch. The front was an inconspicuous brick building with a neon red sign over the doorway. Through the car window I could see a line already formed around the side of the building. Everyone wanted to have a chance at being in the presence of the seductive creatures inside, whether or not they knew what they really were.

"I wish you had worn something less aggressive," my father commented as we stepped out of the limo.

A snort left my nose. "And that fared me so well last night?"

My father led us toward the front door. "They will learn to respect you as they do me. That is what these visits are for."

The bouncer recognized my father right away and stepped aside, opening the velvet rope for us. A few of those in line cried out in protest but were quickly quieted by a murderous look from Gerald.

It took a moment for my eyes to adjust to the dim lighting in the club. Sultry music pulsated through the building, slithering up and into my very veins. My body warmed and a soft touch trailed a hot path across my breasts, making them grow heavy and pebble at the tips. It moved along my skin and settled between my thighs, the music playing a matching beat to the pulsating in my core. I dug my fingers into the palms of my hands until the pain burned through the need to overtake me.

Tricky. Very tricky. To have this much power without ever having to touch a single being. The succubi were merely playing with me back at the mansion. If this was the true extent of their power then I would have to be even more careful than before.

I walked closer to my father and stated, "Until they consider my face alone a threat as they do you, then I will gladly show it in other ways." I adjusted the guns in their holsters, ignoring the strange looks I received by the humans we passed by. "You forget as a woman I will never be seen as someone to fear without shoving it in their faces."

I couldn't hear him clearly over the music and moans, but I could have sworn my father had said, "I never had such a problem with your brothers."

Ignoring his blatant sexism, I kept my eyes forward and off the debauchery around us. Several stages with poles set in the middle of them were spread out around the room. Women and men of all types put on an erotic display for their customers, taking their money and their energy as they crawled around the stage.

Off the stage, even more succubi stalked through the crowds touching someone here and there, spreading their power until the room was just shy of an outright orgy breaking out.

Someone touched me on the ass. Swinging around, I glowered at the man who had dared to put his hands on me. From the haze in his eyes, he was under the succubus's spell and didn't seem too unhappy about it. He chuckled hungrily staring at my breasts then promptly choked on that laugh as his gaze caught sight of my guns. He held his hands up and stumbled backward, falling into the waiting arms of more ready company.

A familiar chuckle reached my ears just barely heard over the music. My head swiveled toward it for more than just one reason.

Azeryth. The very incubus I wanted to see.

I had to hold myself back from going straight to him and beating the answers I wanted out of him. Instead, I held back and leveled my best disinterested glance in his direction.

"Something funny?" I skimmed my eyes over his lounging form. Like a cat, he uncurled himself from the chaise where three women and a man reluctantly released Azeryth so he could stand.

Shirtless but thankfully wearing pants though calling them pants was being nice. The material of said pants clung to every piece of the incubus virtually leaving nothing to the imagination. I kept my gaze on his face and not his still happy bits.

Azeryth dropped down from the upper level to stop in front of me. "Just that you don't let anyone close to you, do you?"

I arched a brow and crossed my arms under my chest. "I would have you know I let plenty close to me, just not you."

He faked a pout, placing a hand over his heart. "You wound me, Madam Van Helsing."

I reminded myself I wasn't here to exchange witty banter with this demon. I was here for answers and now was the time to get them. Stepping toward him, I contemplated if I'd be able to get away with pulling my Colt out in front of all these people. However, before I could try, my father appeared at my side, his hand grabbing my elbow.

"Crysta," his voice firm and unyielding. "We do not have time to play with the peons. Let us not keep our hostess waiting." The words were polite enough but the tightening of his fingers on my elbow sang the threat.

"Of course, father." I gave Azeryth a tight smile and followed after him. Later, I told myself. I'd have plenty of time to talk to Azeryth later.

We made it through the front of the club with little incident after that. My father stopped at a door at the back of the club where another guard stood, this one even more menacing than the last. Though, once more the sight of my father had him stepping to the side and allowing us inside, no questions asked.

When would I instill such fear and respect?

If I had it my way, likely never.

Up a set of stairs to the second floor brought us into a part of the building that was almost exactly like that of below except instead of the tease of intercourse there were full blown orgies being had. The writhing and moaning were almost too much to ignore. The magic that permeated the air even more so.

I dug my nails into my hands once more, keeping my eyes forward as if I would die if I looked elsewhere. Did the succubus leader usually greet my father in such a way? Did he face this level of debauchery every time that he visited? I remembered how unmoved he was by Elise at my celebration party and wondered if it came from centuries of practice. Something my sixty years of life was not prevalent at yet.

Gerald bumped me in the back, and I realized I'd stopped to stare at a particularly engrossing group of people. Only two of them that I could tell were succubi. The rest were humans who were more than happy to be wedged between the other four. The wet sucking and squishing sounds were almost too much for me. I enjoyed sex as much as the next person. There was however such a thing as too much of a good thing. The chaffing alone...I shuddered and kept moving forward that thought enough to keep me from getting distracted again.

Elise, much like her son, lounged on a chaise being hand fed by a group of humans more than happy to peel each and every grape before placing them on her delectably plump lips.

Delectable? Plump lips? What?

Realizing I was being fucked with, I bit the inside of my cheek until I tasted the copper flow of blood.

Elise smiled knowingly in my direction before turning to my father. Unlike her son, she didn't bother standing for my father. And for once I hoped she wouldn't. While at our home she had at least worn something that covered all her important parts. At her own home, Elise didn't bother with practical clothing choosing to wear sheer lingerie that allowed easy access to every inch of her. As she was seated now, I was only shown the impressive expansion of her breasts and I hoped it stayed that way.

"Abraham," Elise purred, holding her hand out to him with a seductive grin. "How thankful we are to have you in our home. After last night's fiasco, I feared we'd get no time together." Her lips pouted just perfectly as she blinked those long lashes at him.

My father, to his credit, was unmoved. He took her hand and pressed a kiss to the back as he would have done back in his younger days. That touch was all that he gave her before dropping it and stepping back. His expression stayed in a neutral position never once giving away what he was thinking.

"My apologies for the disturbance last night," my father acknowledged her complaint, placing one hand over the other in front of his hips. "The shifters' sudden display of aggression was a surprise to all of us."

Head jerking toward my father, I forced my face not to show my surprise. Curious that he would tell her even that much. Was Abraham more affected by her charms than he was letting on or was there something more going on here?

Elise smirked. "We cannot fault the animals for acting as they would. They are, after all, lower beings."

My father went so far as to chuckle. "Yes, well if they were all as civilized as the succubi then my job would be far easier and enjoyable."

Elise flushed with delight.

Ahh. So that was his play.

"And what do you think, Crysta?" Elise turned her attention onto me. "How are you enjoying my home? My son has become quite taken with you."

I resisted the urge to tell her exactly what I thought. My father shot me a warning look as if he knew exactly what I was thinking. However, I surprised them both by saying, "Your home is different...certainly not what I expected. And as for your son..." I paused and cocked one hip to the side with arrogance to rival my father's, "All men want what they can't have."

My father's brows furrowed in anger, but Elise howled with laughter.

"No truer words have been spoken, my child." Elise accepted a glass of liquid from one of her humans, taking a sip before patting the chaise next to her. "Please come sit with me for a while."

The grimace that fought to creep up my face was a hard-won battle against the neutral expression that ended up winning instead. Without a look at my father or the humans in various stages of undress, I sat down beside her keeping as much distance between us as possible.

"Oh, don't be so shy," Elise purred, wrapping an arm around my waist, effectively closing the distance between us. "I can tell we're going to be great friends, you and I, Crysta." She played with the curls of my hair, wrapping and unwrapping it around one of her long fingers. "You know, when your father mentioned he'd be stepping down I'd been worried your brother would take over."

I stiffened. Was she about to admit doing something to Michael?

"Mickey was such a loyal customer until he found love," she said the word with such disdain that I had to hold back my own retort. "Now it's all about keeping boundaries. No fun at all. Not like your father." She licked her lips and blew a kiss in Abraham's direction. Turning back to me, she frowned. "You're so stiff. Relax. I won't bite."

I didn't. And I was quite sure that she would. "No offense meant but you're not my type."

Elise cocked her head to the side. "Not your type? I'm everyone's type. Are you not into females?" When I didn't answer, she stared at me for a long moment before turning to my father. "How old is she again?"

My father who had been watching this interaction with a guarded expression simply stated, "Her sixtieth birthday was last night."

"Oh, right." Elise clucked her tongue and turned back to me to smile with pity. "You're still a baby. Do not worry, young Crysta. I can show you the pleasures men and women can give you." She stroked a long nail down my arm causing the skin to pebble with her power.

Not liking how this conversation was going, I stood abruptly. They had to know I was the new power even if I didn't plan to keep it. Elise almost fell into the spot that I had vacated and stared up at me with surprise.

"I may be young," I retorted with a firm tone, "But I still have standards. When I say you are not my type, it is not your gender or even your looks." I gestured to her voluptuous form. "It's the hatefulness and haughtiness in your heart that is not to my taste."

My father started to interrupt me.

I held a hand up. "No, if I'm to be your heir then they must know how things will be between us." Turning my attention back to Elise, I stared straight into those big green eyes. "I am not your plaything, and I will not be treated as such. I am your equal. I will do my best to be just and fair in all manners of issues that arise. I give you honesty now so that you may give me the same in return when the time comes that I have to come to you about one of your own."

"Crysta!" My father stepped in front of me blocking me off from Elise. "Elise, I apologize for my daughter's outburst—"

"No," Elise interrupted him with a wave of her hand. "She's correct. I cannot expect my relationship with Crysta to be the same as it was with you. I appreciate your honesty and accept your conditions. Please," she offered me her hand with a genuine smile, "let us start again."

I placed my hand in hers and shook it. "It would be my pleasure."

CHAPTER 11

AFTER SETTLING THINGS WITH Elise, the encounter was actually pleasant in a way. I mean, if you could ignore the orgies going on around you enough to have a decent conversation.

She asked me about my time in the human world and I asked about how her business worked. My father stood to the side the entire time with a blank expression that no doubt meant he was not happy. Oh, well. Couldn't please everyone.

"I have to say," Elise led me through the room to the exit, "I had a more enjoyable time than I originally thought."

"Me too," I admitted, and it was actually true.

"Perhaps we could meet again some time?" Elise asked, her question showing a vulnerability in her that I hadn't seen yet before my father.

I smiled at her and nodded. "I'd like that but maybe..." I shot a look behind her trying not to grimace. "Somewhere less crowded."

Elise laughed, her head thrown back and her long blonde hair falling over her shoulders. "Agreed." She turned to my father and inclined her head, "Abraham."

"Elise." My father's tone was indecipherable. Whether or not it bothered Elise, she didn't show it.

I took the stairs back down to the main floor, not allowing my father's blatant stare at my back bother me. We were silent all the way to the limo until I stopped at the curb.

"I'm going to hang around for a while," I informed my father and Gerald.

My father paused at the door, holding it with his hand. "I would think you'd had your fill of this environment already."

I couldn't hold back my grimace this time. "While it isn't my preferred form of entertainment, I believe it is important to be amongst the supernaturals so that they will be more willing to come forward when the time comes."

He stared at me for a long moment and then shook his head. "You are something else, daughter."

I arched my brow. "I'm not sure if that is a compliment or an insult."

"Neither," he corrected. "You are doing things in a different way than I would have and I'm not sure if it is a good thing or a bad thing. However, it seems to be working so I will allow it." He slid into the limo without another word and Gerald closed the door behind him.

I scowled at the limo and watched as it drove away, leaving me on the curb alone. "I'll allow it," I mimicked his words with a sneer. Fucking right he would. I wasn't going to rule the way that he did faking friends while plotting their demise behind their backs. I'd never been very good at the political game the way he and my brothers were, and I wasn't going to pretend to be. I would play to my strengths and that was making friends.

Turning back to the club, I sucked in a breath. Now that business has concluded I could focus on what I'd really come here for.

Azeryth.

The bouncer opened the rope for me once more, gaining me just as many protests from those waiting in line. I ignored them and walked back inside. This time I wasn't surprised by the magic pressing against my skin and brushed it off as I searched the crowd for my target.

Coming here alone to confront Azeryth was probably not the smartest idea. Good thing I had a plan.

Pulling my phone out, I shot a group text off to Jerrod and Ines, informing them of my plan so if things went wrong, they could come running.

One hour. **Ines text back**. If I don't hear from you in an hour, I'm sending the Calvary.

I'll be fine, I sent back and shoved my phone into my rear pocket.

I had to hurry. Knowing Ines, it wasn't an idle threat. I'd have an hour, maybe less, to find Azeryth and get the information I needed out of him.

This time, instead of stalking through the room, I made my way to an empty low table with a U-shaped couch around it. I could have approached Azeryth right away, I'd spotted him at the same table as before, tongue deep in the mouth of the handsome human beside him. However, if I wanted to catch him off guard, I couldn't be the one to come to him. He'd suspect something for sure.

A pretty - aren't they all? - succubus with bright red hair in a pale green thong and pasties over her nipples came to my table. She smiled shyly in my direction, her eyes flickering to my guns. "Want company?"

I couldn't tell if the shy approach she was taking was for real or fake which meant she was good. I offered her a polite smile and shook my head. Then pulled a card out and placed it on the table. "Can I get a gin and tonic? Thank you."

The redhead took my card and turned towards the bar not put off by my denial. Three more succubi - male and female - came by my table before the redhead came back with my drink.

"They're going to keep coming until someone sits with you," the waitress informed me, setting my drink on the table.

I wrapped my hand around the glass and brought it to settle in front of me. "Well, then I guess I have no choice. Please," I gestured to the space next to me. The redhead sat down, politely keeping her distance from me. "What's your name?"

"Elle," the succubus said, leaning forward on her elbows so that her breasts were pushed up in the best possible position.

I held out my hand, keeping my eyes on her face. "Hello, Elle. I'm Crysta Van Helsing."

Immediately, her pale blue eyes widened, and she hesitantly took my hand. "Uh, hi. I didn't do anything. Are you here to arrest someone?"

I shook my head. "Relax. I'm just getting a feel for your kind. I've been playing human for a while and wanted to get to know the succubi better."

"Oh," Elle's brows lifted. Then she offered me a seductive grin, her hand on mine turning sensual. I could feel the magic pushing across my skin.

I cocked my head to the side. "Do you always do that?"

Startled by my question, Elle's magic faltered. "Do what?"

"Try to seduce anyone you deem a threat."

Elle's face flushed. "I - I don't do that."

I lifted my glass to my lips once more and took a long drink giving her time to collect herself. "It's alright. I'm not going to punish you for it. You aren't breaking any rules.

Besides, if I had all my bits out in such a vulnerable position, I'd be defensive too."

She shrugged. "I don't see it as being vulnerable. My body is my biggest weapon. I can bring men and women to their knees. I can make more money here using my body than I could at any white-collar job, and I get to be who I am instead of pretending to be what they want me to be."

"They?"

"The rest of the world." Elle jerked her head toward the doorway where a group of humans came in laughing. "They come here not knowing what we are and yet accepting us nonetheless because we give them something they want. There's no lies. No reason to pretend. Just pleasure." She trailed her hand over her collar bone causing one of the male humans to pause with his friends and stare at her with open lust. Then as sudden as she had captured him, she dropped her hand and turned back to me. "You can't imagine the rush such a power has."

"That's a side I'd never thought of before." I sat my drink back on the table and turned to her. "Can you do it without your powers?"

She peered at me, curiosity creeping into her eyes. "You mean can I pull someone without using my abilities on them?" I nodded. "Oh, sure. Our magic just enhances the attraction; we can't just create it out of thin air."

I bobbed my head along with her words. Good to know. So, I only had to figure out a way not to be attracted to any of them and then their powers won't work on me at all. Ha. Like that was possible.

Knowing my time was running out, I contemplated how I would get Azeryth to notice me so I could put my new friend's words to the test. I could use something other than violence to get what I wanted. After all, Azeryth would expect violence...

"Would you like to try it?"

"Huh?" I blinked at Elle. "Try what?"

"To see how it feels to have all eyes on you. It's more liberating than you would think." Elle leaned closer to me, an eager gleam in her eyes.

Hmmm. All eyes, huh? This may work.

"I don't have to take my clothes off, do I?" I squinted at her with a frown.

Elle laughed. "No. Not at all. Though it helps. I would just get rid of the guns. They don't exactly send the right signal."

I glanced down at the twin Colts on either side of my breasts and pursed my lips. She had a point. However, being a Van Helsing with the only weapon who could kill us it would be ill advised to give it up, whether or not they knew I could die from just a regular old butter knife.

For a moment, I contemplated the risk and reward. Did I really want to go this route to get information on my brother's kidnapper? I could go around this another way and just threaten it out of Azeryth. However...I talked of trust to Elise, so I had to put my words on the line and prove that I wasn't just all talk.

Sighing, I unhooked the leather holding the holster in place and laid it on the table. Elle placed a hand on them and clicked her fingers in the air. A large man with long black hair appeared at our table.

"Don't worry, Edgar will take good care of them, promise." She handed my gun holster and all over to the large man who inclined his head and walked back to the bar where he placed my weapons in a vault.

"Come on," Elle held a hand out to me and drew me out of the booth. Hand in hand we strolled through the crowd gaining more and more attention as we made our way to the main stage. Elle led me to the stairs and paused, gesturing for me to go up.

I stared at the pole with wide eyes. Sixty years old and I'd rather stare down the barrel of a gun than dance on that pole in front of all these people.

"Just close your eyes and go for it," Elle murmured to me, giving me a little push. "Don't think about the crowd yet. Just let the music do the talking."

I blew out a harsh breath. Better said than done. Trying to keep my eyes on the pole and not at those crowding around the stage, I curled and uncurled my fingers. I could do this. I was trained in all forms of martial arts. This was just like that...kind of.

My fingers wrapped around the pole, and I closed my eyes. Cheers and shouts of encouragement were sent my way which only served to make me more nervous than confident.

I could do this. Just feel the music.

The beat roamed along my skin and warmed my blood. I swayed from one side to the other, getting a feel for the music. Each beat made me bolder, more confident, and then the room fell away, and I just danced. I undulated my hips to the music, pressing myself against the pole allowing the cool metal to comfort me and push me on. Dropping down to the ground, I arched my back as I came back up, gaining myself a chorus of cheers.

Hesitantly, I opened my eyes and peered out into the crowd. There weren't any people jeering at me or telling me to get off the stage. In fact, every single person was staring at me with lust in their eyes. It surprised me so much that I almost fell off the stage in my effort to get down.

Elle met me at the bottom, giggling as she patted me on the back. "Almost perfect. Need to work on your exit though."

I ducked my head and dragged a hand through my hair. "Uh, yeah. But I get what you meant. It was definitely different than what I expected."

"I'm glad you were so willing to try it." Elle responded with pride. "Most Van Helsings would have been too full of themselves to put themselves in our shoes."

"Crysta is like no Van Helsing I've ever known." Elle and I turned toward Azeryth, who leaned against the stage railing staring at me like he was seeing me in a whole new light now.

Elle placed a hand on my arm and squeezed. "I better get back to work. Hope to see you again."

"Me too. Thanks." I waved to her and then turned toward the one I had been trying to attract. Seemed my plan had worked now to reel him in and get what I wanted out of him. Turning my back to him, I walked through the crowd accepting compliments and declining invitations all the while knowing Azeryth was following me. I stopped at the bar where I picked up my weapons. I took my time sliding the holster back on, allowing Azeryth time to catch up to me.

"I've been hearing quite a few things about you, Crysta Van Helsing." Azeryth announced beside me.

I arched a brow and snapped my holster back into place. "Oh yeah? Like what?"

"Things that don't sound very Van Helsing like." Azeryth placed a toothpick between his teeth and swished it from one side to the other. "Are you sure you're one of them?"

Huffing a laugh, I shook my head and walked to the door. As I'd hoped Azeryth followed me. If I had to get rough, I didn't want to do it on succubus grounds. It would completely destroy the new foundation I was trying to set up.

I continued out the door and down the street, passing all the humans still waiting to get into the club. It was already close to midnight and still they came.

The sound of Azeryth's designer shoes stomped on the sidewalk behind me as I passed in and out of the streetlights. He wasn't as stealthy as the video portrayed him to be. Or was it a ruse? Could this really be the same man who had left an eyeball as a gift in Ines's room?

"Wait up," Azeryth called out, slightly out of breath. "I want to talk to you."

I paused and turned around, smirking at the out of breath incubus. "For all those rippling pectorals you sure skimp out on the cardio, huh?"

"Hey, I get plenty of cardio. It's just usually more..." he flexed his hips, "...stationary."

"Got it." Bobbing my head, I continued walking backward. "You want to talk. Talk."

"What were you doing here?" Azeryth began catching me off guard.

"You mean besides visiting your mother like a good little heir?" I shrugged. "I wanted to see what the fuss was about."

Azeryth cocked a brow. "So, it wasn't to question why I was sneaking out of the mansion this morning?"

I stumbled a step and almost landed on my ass when Azeryth was suddenly there, his arms wrapped around my waist keeping me up. "Thanks." I pushed him away and stepped back. "Okay, so you do know you were being shady as fuck."

He shrugged, not at all guilty in his smirk. "What can I say? I like to play with the line."

"Enough to send body parts to a grieving fiancé?" I countered with a snarl.

Azeryth's squinted at me and pulled back. "Wait, what? Body parts? What body parts?"

"Don't play dumb now," I shoved a finger at his chest closing the distance between us. "You put that box in Ines's room, didn't you?"

He held his hands up and frowned. "What box? Who's Ines?"

"Now I know you're lying." I growled wishing he was wearing a shirt I could grab him by. "Everyone knows that Ines was engaged to my brother, Michael."

"Michael?" Azeryth lowered his hands and frowned. "I've never even met your brother. I've been off running our other clubs around the country. Why would I send anything to his fiancé? Is this something to do with why he died?"

I promptly closed my mouth and stepped back. I was wrong or Azeryth is a better liar than I gave him credit for. "Why were you sneaking around the mansion then?"

Azeryth dragged a hand through his hair, a sheepish grin on his face. "Banging some Van Helsings, of course. You can get as rough as you want with your kind without worrying you'll die on me."

I gaped at him. "You...you..."

"Hey, don't knock it until you try it." Azeryth scowled, crossing his arms over his chest. "Now that I answered your question, answer mine."

I almost didn't. I almost kept him in the dark and went home. Then that little voice in the back of my head. The one that had me standing up to his mother rather than letting her think she was getting her way came roaring back to the front.

"Michael was taken. We don't know who took him and my father refuses to search for him or show the supernaturals any weakness. Even if it means getting little bits of his son back in boxes." My rage at my father leaked into my words and I was sure that Azeryth heard it. I didn't care. I wanted my brother back and I wanted him back now.

"I'm sorry to hear about your brother," Azeryth told me, and from what I could tell he was sincere. "I wish I could tell you something. Help you in some way but I don't know anything. I didn't even see anyone when I was leaving this morning."

"What about at the club?" I tried, hoping against hope that I could get some lead...any. Cause if Azeryth wasn't behind it then I was back to square one. Which was nowhere.

Azeryth shook his head sadly. "I haven't heard anything. But I can make some inquiries. Discretely of course."

I narrowed my eyes on him. "And what do you want in return?"

Smirking, Azeryth held his hand out to me. "Just the same offer you gave my mother. Friends, equals, rather than a tyrant ruler."

I stared at his hand for half a beat before placing mine in it. "Agreed."

Not even a second after I touched my hand to his then did the hair on the back of my neck stand on end. I grabbed a hold of Azeryth's hand and jerked him toward me, "Get down!"

CHAPTER 12

SHOTS FIRE WHERE WE had stood just moments ago. Azeryth gasped and the crowd of humans not more than a block from us screamed and scattered.

"Get up, get up," I shouted to Azeryth, pulling him by the same hand racing us toward the shadows of a nearby alley. A sharp pain pierced my side, but I couldn't stop now.

"They're shooting at us!" He hissed, clinging to me but thankfully drawing more attention to us.

"Yeah, I noticed." I pushed him further back into the alley and unholstered both Colts, trying to ignore the pain and liquid drenching the inside of my corset.

"Why?"

I shrugged. "Why does anybody try to kill anyone?"

"You think they want to kill us?" Azeryth grabbed my arm and jerked me around, gaining a grunt of pain from me.

Shaking him loose, I focused my senses on the direction the shots had come from. "Kill us, kidnap us, send pieces back to our loved ones. Who knows nowadays?"

"That's not funny."

"It wasn't meant to be," I shot over my shoulder before inching toward the edge of the brick wall. Shots hit the corner just above my head sending dirt and pieces of wall spraying down on us.

Shit.

"Why don't you just go out there, guns blazing like in the movies? You're virtually indestructible, aren't you?" Azeryth asked close behind me. "At least give me a chance to run back to the club."

I scoffed. "You've never been in a fight before, have you?"

Azeryth straightened and brushed his thumb against his nose. "Well, you know...I'm more of a lover than a fighter."

I snorted. "Obviously. In any case, I don't know if they have Van Helsing made weapons, do you?"

"Well, uh, no I don't. Can't you tell?" Azeryth peeked toward the edge of the alley. I pushed him back just before the shots were fired once more. At this rate the local authorities would come. If you could count on the humans for one thing it was calling for help whether it was wanted or not.

"No, I can't tell," I snapped, pushing us further back into the alley. To my dismay, there wasn't an exit to the alley, only more brick walls and the back of the other building.

"So, you've all been going out to fight without knowing if your enemies had the very weapons that they needed to kill you?"

I turned away from the dead end and lifted my hands, shrugging. "Doesn't everyone do that? It's not that big of a deal."

"Except most people don't have a fifty-fifty chance of surviving the injury," Azeryth pointed out.

"More like twenty-eighty since the likelihood they have any of our weapons are low. We do keep them closely guarded…" I added to myself, "…usually."

"We're trapped." Azeryth finally noticed, searching around the alley like a bug caught in a cup. "What are we going to do? They're going to kill us."

Shaking off the blood loss making my head woozy, I pointed my Colts at the entrance to the alley way and let that cool white noise take over my mind. "Not if we kill them first."

"Wait, what?"

Ignoring Azeryth's whimpering, I focused on the end of the alley. When a figure stepped into the shadows, my fingers were poised and ready to squeeze the trigger. Then when I thought this was the end, Jerrod's familiar head appeared in the alleyway with Ines close behind.

"Oh, thank fuck," I gasped before blacking out.

"What the fuck do you mean I can't see her?" a high-pitched voice pierced my ears before I had barely regained consciousness.

"You should be merely happy that you are even allowed on the property," a snooty voice countered with a low growl. A growl I recognized. Azeryth. What was he still doing here?

"Look here, buster," the first voice snapped. "I'm Crysta's best friend. Best. Friend. Got that? That means everything about her matters to me. And if she's been shot, I very damn well am going to be by her side when she wakes up. You got me?"

It clicked in my brain who the first voice was. It took me a moment to realize it because the very thought that Bethany would be here of all places was just unfathomable. She should be safe at school, not in the infirmary of the Van Helsing's mansion, where I assumed I was at.

Letting my eyes slit open, I groaned at the sudden brightness above me.

"She's awake!" Bethany cried, followed by a thud. "Get out of my way." Bethany grasped my hand and her shadow covered up some of the light above me allowing me to open my eyes fully. "Crysta? Can you hear me? Do you hurt anywhere?"

I huffed a laugh and then hissed. A stinging ache ripped through my side. Oh, yeah. I was shot.

"If you're laughing that means you can't be that hurt," Bethany confirmed with a smile. Her blonde hair flowed over her shoulders and framed her face, a trail of happy tears sliding down her face. "Don't ever do that to me again, you hear me?" She pushed at my shoulder making me rock in the infirmary bed.

"Ouch, geez. I'm still hurt here, you know." I reminded her with a wince. "What are you doing here?"

Bethany scowled and narrowed her eyes on me. "I go out of my way to make sure you're not dead or dying and the first thing you ask is what am I doing here? What kind of best friend are you?"

"The kind that expected you to call rather than show up at her doorstep," Gerald's voice appeared somewhere in the room.

I angled my head to the side trying to see around Bethany. "What kind of bodyguard are you? You were supposed to give her my number so she didn't think I was dead, not bring her home with you."

"Hey, don't blame Gerald." Bethany snapped her fingers in front of my face to gain my attention. "I didn't accept that you had just lost your phone. I wanted to see you for myself. So I forced Gerald to lead me here."

"More like followed me," Gerald grumbled.

I laughed again, grabbing my side as the pain became too much. "Please, don't make me laugh."

"Ohhh," Bethany whined, waving her hands frantically over me. "I'm sorry. Uh...isn't there any painkillers you can give her?" She asked Quinn.

"Not that she hasn't already had."

"How did you get shot anyway?" Bethany turned her attention back to me with a frown. "This isn't exactly the south. Who carries guns around all willy nilly?"

I shook my head. "It's a long story." To Gerald, I asked, "Does my father know what's happened?"

Gerald inclined his head. "Yes, Jerrod and Ines gave him a full report as soon as they came back with you and this one." He pointed at Azeryth.

I glanced at the incubus and frowned. "Why didn't you go home?"

Azeryth scowled and gestured a hand toward the doorway. "Your cousins wouldn't let me go home until they made sure that I wasn't the target or in on the attack."

"Fucking wow," Bethany gaped at them. "What kind of world do you live in, Crysta?"

I pushed myself up on my elbows and winced. "One that's not up for discussion right now. Gerald, will you find a room for Bethany, please?"

"Your father isn't going to be happy about a hum - her being here," Gerald informed me, scanning over Bethany.

"My father can suck it," I grimaced and then turned to Azeryth. "Have you called your mother yet?" He shook his head. "You should probably do that before your mother thinks we kidnapped you and one missing person is enough for me right now."

"Wait, what? Who's been kidnapped?" Bethany questioned as Gerald ushered her out of the room. "Come on, Gerald. Don't hold out on me now."

When she left the room, I sighed heavily. One thing at a time. First off. I searched for Quinn. When I found her, I gestured to Azeryth. "Will you let him use your phone to call home? I doubt he has one in those..." I surveyed his tight-fitting bottoms and arched a brow in question, "...pants?"

Azeryth smirked. "Yeah, nope. No pockets in these babies."

Quinn handed over the cordless phone in the infirmary to Azeryth, who took the phone and stepped over to the side. When he was out of hearing range, I turned back to Quinn. "So, what's the verdict?"

A firm press of lips was all I needed to know but Quinn said it anyway for me. "You're lucky it didn't hit any vital organs. I got the bullet out before anyone could see that it wasn't one of ours. Either way, you're going to live."

"Thanks," I grunted. "The last thing I need is for the son of succubi to know about my condition. Though, it sucks that I didn't get the instant healing bits."

Quinn gave me a tight smile. "Just be glad you heal faster than humans or you'd be out of commission for tonight's events."

I groaned and threw an arm over my forehead. "He's still going to make me go through with it?"

Shrugging, Quinn glanced over my wound while Azeryth was still distracted. "You know your father. If you're not on death's doorstep then you still have to work. Don't think because you're his daughter that makes you special."

I snorted. "Never did."

Quinn handed me a pill bottle. "That's what I like about you. You know exactly what you are and never pretend to be otherwise. Take two every six hours until the pain subsides. It goes without saying that alcohol is out of the question."

"Yeah, yeah." I took the bottle and inched my legs over the side of the bed. I hissed out a breath of air though it did little to reduce my pain. This whole situation was just going from bad to worse. First, I get absolutely fucking nowhere with Azeryth. Then I get shot and now Bethany was here. What else could possibly go wrong?

"Here you go," Azeryth handed the phone back to Quinn. "I let my mother know that I decided to come back with you for a little 'get to know me time.'" He wagged his brows. My fist darted out before I could second guess it and slammed into his stomach, knocking the air out of him. "What the fuck was that for?"

"For implying that I would ever sleep with you." I pushed up from the bed and took a few hesitant steps forward. When I didn't collapse and the pain was bearable, I continued out of the infirmary with Azeryth close on my heels.

"You wouldn't?" Azeryth asked curiously as if someone had never told him such a thing before.

I shot him a look, staying close to the wall. I didn't touch it so I could hide how injured I actually was from the incubus, but I wanted it there just in case I couldn't hold myself up any longer.

"Unlike you, I have standards and they don't include someone who would ever wear something..." I skimmed my gaze over the skintight bottoms and his thankfully flaccid bits. "...so ostentatious."

"Ahhh, so you're a prude."

I stopped before the stairs and blew a hard breath through my nose. "I may be young compared to some, but that doesn't mean that I have to flaunt my sexuality or bedroom activities everywhere I go. My job is to keep your kind in line. If I allowed myself to be seduced so easily what would the others think of me? I would lose their respect as well as any foot hold I have tried to gain in the last few days."

Turning away from him, I gritted my teeth as I faced the long trek up the stairs.

"That must suck."

I paused on the first step, not turning back to him. "What?"

"Having to hide who you are so much for the sake of the rest of us." Azeryth's tone wasn't teasing or condescending, and it made me actually shift back around to him.

"There is more to this position than just telling everyone else what to do, you know. Everyone has their parts to play regardless if we want to play them." I gripped the banister beneath my hand. "I long ago gave up the idea that I could just be who I wanted to be. I'm a Van Helsing and nothing and no one will change that."

Azeryth huffed. "Still, it makes me feel like I need to do better. Be more mature or something." He laced his fingers behind his head and stared up at the ceiling for a long moment. Then he snorted and threw his head back and laughed. "Nah. I'll leave that for you stiff types."

I smiled despite myself. "Fine with me. But I'd head home if I were you."

"No way," Azeryth puffed, hands on his hips. "How do we know they weren't trying to kill me?"

He had a point. "We don't. So, I guess you can stay here. Just don't make a nuisance of yourself."

"Like I would?" Azeryth smirked, and then glanced around him. "Which way is it to the kitchens? I'm starved."

I pointed around the stairway to the back hall. "Down that way and to the left. But I'm warning you, the only thing you better be eating is food or Ana will get you."

Azeryth cocked his head to the side. "I think I can take care of myself."

I started my trek back up the stairs and waved a feeble hand over my shoulder. "Don't say I didn't warn you."

Once Azeryth was gone, I continued my agonizing trek up the stairs. Normally, I'd ask for help or stay in the infirmary. However, since Azeryth and Bethany were around, I couldn't let them know how injured I actually was. While I wasn't sure what Azeryth would do with the information, I knew Bethany would freak out and refuse to leave my side. I didn't need that right now.

I loved my best friend. I did. However, her being here right now was horrible, horrible timing. How was I going to create a relationship with the supernatural community, figure out who has my brother, and protect Bethany from it all?

Then there was the whole question of should I tell her what was really happening or leave her in the dark.

Fuck, my head was hurting from all this. I just wanted to lay down and rest for a bit. Then I could sort it all out later.

I eased down the hallway, keeping my eyes on a space in the distance. No one tried to talk to me, and I couldn't appreciate it more. If I had to do small talk right now, I might just kill someone.

Finally in my room, I collapsed against the door. I took a moment to breathe in and out slowly so as not to pull on my stitches. With how often I got injured, one would think that I'd be used to the pain by now.

No such luck.

Pain was like anything else in life. Ongoing and you never knew which way it would take you. This one wouldn't take me to the death bed. However, better to take precautions than to leave it to fate.

Pushing up off the door, I shuffled over to my bed. I eased down onto the mattress and closed my eyes, letting myself get through the pain before leaning over to sit my pain meds on the nightstand.

I stopped.

There on my nightstand sat a box. A shoe box. There was no label showing where the shoes had come from or a note on the outside for me to see the sender.

Somewhere in the back of my mind something told me not to open it. That I should leave it where it was and go get Jerrod. However, I was partly human, and my curiosity got the best of me.

Reaching over, I placed the pills down and picked up the box. It wasn't heavy like a pair of shoes which should have been my first sign to put it back.

I sat the box in my lap and stared down at it for a long moment. Grasping the sides of the lid, I inched the box open as if it were a jack in the box about to spring on me. Thankfully, nothing jumped out and there was a note on top of a bundle of dark red tissue wrapping paper.

Pursing my lips, I unfolded the note and peered down at it.

I heard you were looking for me. Let me give you a hand.

That didn't bode well. Placing the note to the side, I pulled one side of the tissue paper away, frowning at the wetness of it and then the other side. I shoved the box onto the bed and flopped over the side, throwing up everything in my stomach. Since I'd been out for a while it wasn't much. Water, maybe a bit of the alcohol from last night, and then it was just dry heaves.

When I finished, I swiped the side of my mouth with the back of my hand and glanced over at the box where a hand with the Van Helsing crest tattooed on the top sat in a puddle of blood.

CHAPTER 13

A KNOCK SOUNDED AT my door before it opened, Ines poking her head inside. "Crysta? I was just coming to check on...what are you doing?" She pursed her lips and walked toward me, leaving the door wide open. "Did you pull your stitches already?"

I grunted, my hand on my side. Then my eyes caught sight of the box next to me and I jerked to my feet. "No, Ines..." I groaned as pain ripped through my side. Still, I was determined not to have Ines see what was in the box.

"Jeez, Crysta," Ines grabbed for me, trying to usher me back down onto the bed. "Ew," she grumbled when she sidestepped my vomit. "You made yourself throw up already? You need to take it easy. Do you have a death wish or something?"

"No, I just-"

Ines wasn't listening to me. "Did you forget we have a human and an incubus in the manor? Do you want the enemy to learn of your secret? Or worry Bethany? I mean..." she bent over to check my stitches, "...what's that? A gift?" Ines reached for the box, and I shoved her away.

"No, Ines. Don't."

Frowning, Ines pushed my hands away. "What's the big idea? Is it something embarrassing? Come on, you can show me," she grinned, reaching for the box again, "I'm practically your sister any...way..."

I turned my head away not wanting to see the look of horror on her face when she realized what was in the box. Unfortunately, I didn't need to see her reaction. A gut-wrenching scream poured from Ines's mouth, making me wince.

The balcony doors slammed open and even without looking, I knew the guards from below had popped in. The bedroom door shoved open even further as three others appeared in the doorway, weapons at ready.

I waved them off as I casually pushed myself back up on the bed and closed the lid on the shoe box. "False alarm, guys. No need to call in the Calvary."

The three in the doorway stared at me and then at Ines before exchanging a worried look. One of them, Timothy, I think, stepped forward with concern on his face. "Ines? Is everything okay?"

Ines had gone into some kind of catatonic state after I had closed the shoe box. Her mouth gaped open, and she blinked at the bed where the shoebox sat. I wrapped an arm around the box and shoved it behind me, cutting off her line of sight. As if a spell had broken, Ines shook her head rubbing the side of her face.

"Ines?" Timothy asked again.

"Uh, yeah. I'm fine." she tossed her hair over her shoulder and nodded as if to confirm to herself. "Yes, I'm good. Just uh..." Ines locked eyes with me and I shook my head giving her a meaningful look. "...I just, you know, saw a spider...yeah a spider..."

A cough that sounded like it was covering up a laugh came from one of the guards by the balcony. Ines glared at them. "You think that's funny?"

"No, no," the guard shook their head, standing up straight. "Of course not, ma'am."

Ines pushed to her feet, placing her fists on her hips. "Then don't you have somewhere to be?"

The rest of the guards straightened as well before nodding their heads and disappearing out the balcony as quickly as they came. Once they were gone, Ines turned that icy gaze on the three others at the door. "Well?"

Timothy pursed his lips. His eyes shone with suspicion. Still, he turned on his heels and left with the others closing the door behind them.

When they were gone, I sagged on the bed clutching my side and groaning. "Fuck. I definitely pulled some stitches."

Ines rushed to my side, lifting the side of my shirt to check the bleeding coming through my bandage. "Yeah. You're gonna have to go back to the medic but first..." she reached around me and grabbed the box before I could stop her. "What the fuck is this?"

I slapped my hand on top of the box before she could open it again. "Don't. It's exactly what it looks like, and it won't make you feel any better seeing it a second time."

Swallowing down the fear in her eyes, Ines met my gaze. "Why didn't you want them to see it?"

"Because," I grimaced and shifted off the edge of the bed to a staggering stance. I leaned against the bedpost for balance. "I'm starting to think this is an inside job and I don't know who I can trust."

Ines's brown eyes widened. "An inside job? Why?"

I tapped the top of the box. "Who else would get into my bedroom without setting off the alarm? Your room, fine. But the heir's?" I shook my head. "You saw how fast they showed up just from your screaming. Also," I pushed off the bedpost and forced myself to stand tall. "I don't think it was Azeryth. If you'd seen him during the attack last night, you'd know right away he wouldn't have the stomach for this." I gestured at the box.

"I don't blame him," Ines muttered, a bit green in the gills. She gripped the box tightly in her hands, pressing it to her chest as if she had Michael right there with her. "What do we do now? Do we tell your father?"

"No, not yet. I need to check on something." I stepped toward the door and then stopped. "I'll send Jerrod down here to sit with you."

Ines glowered. "You mean babysit me. I'm not going to freak out again."

I arched my brow.

"I won't," Ines insisted. She stared down at the box in her hands. "Look, I know I can't use my 'I'm his fiancé' excuse since you're his sister and you're not freaking out."

"I did throw up though," I pointed out behind her.

Ines scrunched her nose up at the mess. "Yeah, good point. Anyway, shouldn't you go to the infirmary first?"

"I'll go there after I get Jerrod." Ines gave me a look. "I promise. Okay."

"Fine, but if I find you passed out in the hallway, don't come crying to me."

I paused at the bedroom door and frowned. "I won't, cause I'll be unconscious."

Ines waved a hand in the air. "You know what I mean."

"Yeah, yeah. Don't open that box." I pointed at the container she was clutching so tightly. "I mean it, Ines. Just don't."

I didn't wait for her to respond before walking out the door. I promised I'd go to the infirmary, and I would. However, I didn't trust Ines alone with that box for long. It was better to have someone there with her to keep her from breaking down again.

Keeping my hand on the wall as I moved down the corridor, I tried to keep a neutral expression. It wouldn't do for Bethany or even Azeryth to see me now. For that matter, the rest of the clan shouldn't see me either. What would they say if they saw their would-be leader collapsed in the hallway?

I stopped and sighed. Maybe I should have just sent Ines to get Jerrod. Blowing out a long breath, I huffed a laugh. "Yeah, right. Like she'd give up that box."

"What box?"

My head jerked around to the voice. Eric stared at me, his brows bunched together, worry lighting his eyes.

"Oh, nothing. Just talking to myself." I made myself straighten up more even though it hurt.

Still, Eric's watchful eyes latched on to every movement. "Should you be walking around in your condition?"

I stiffened. In my condition? Suspicion rose in me as I locked my gaze with his. "And what condition would that be?"

Eric grinned sheepishly and waved his hands before him. "No offense meant. I just mean you're bleeding through your shirt. Is that okay?"

My gaze dipped down to my wound where it had indeed soaked through the material. I covered it with my hand and turned my head away. "I'm fine. Did you want something?"

"Oh, okay. If you're sure." Eric's tone countered his words not sounding like he was dropping it at all. "Anyway, your father asked me to send you his way. It seems he received a present as well."

My eyes widened and I jerked my head back around to him. "A present? You mean a box? What was in it?"

Eric stepped back as I moved toward him, shaking his head. "I don't know. It's the same kind of box but I didn't get to see what was inside. I was just delivering the daily reports and Abraham asked me to pass on the message."

I grunted. "Alright. I'll be along shortly. Thanks." Turning away from him, I focused on getting to Jerrod's room rather than the eyes on my back.

This wasn't good. Two boxes in one day? Were they getting impatient? Or was it all part of their sick game?

I didn't know. The one thing I did know was that I couldn't do anything until I took care of my part first, then I'd see to Father.

By some miracle, no one else stopped me and I didn't pass out from blood loss. The latter was more likely at this point. I stopped before Jerrod's door and raised my hand to knockbut paused my hand as I heard a grunt and then a hiss.

"No, don't."

I didn't wait any longer. I threw the door open prepared to come to Jerrod's aid. Except what I got was an image I never wanted to be embedded into my head.

Standing in front of his bed, Jerrod held Azeryth by the back of the neck, his tongue down his throat. The incubus didn't seem to mind as much so the earlier protest from Jerrod must have been some kind of game.

Jerrod's pants were undone, and his shirt was disheveled while Azeryth's shirt had completely disappeared. The incubus's pants sat below the swell of his ass, his cock exposed and being pumped by Jerrod's hand.

The bastards didn't even bother to stop in my presence. Or maybe they didn't notice I was there...

"Are you just going to keep watching like some big pervert?" Jerrod asked, a smirk on his face while he pumped Azeryth's cock faster.

"Ugh, come on." I turned my face to the side, my cheeks burning. "If you knew I was there then why didn't you stop."

Jerrod chuckled. "If it was important enough for you to come barging in then I'm not inclined to stop what I'm doing until I hear you out."

Azeryth groaned and panted out, "Aren't you guys like cousins? I mean, I might be a incubus but that's pushing it even for us." He let out a strangled cry and my eyes jerked to Jerrod's hand before I could stop it in time to see Azeryth cum all over Jerrod's hand.

Lifting the hand, Jerrod smirked before licking the side of his hand. "Only in the sense that all of us are cousins in some way or another. I lost track after the fifth twice removed crap. Right, Crysta?"

I gulped and forced my eyes to the ceiling. "Yeah. I guess."

"So, you have guys ever..." Azeryth began, cut off by Bethany crying out, "Crysta, you're bleeding!"

My hand went to my side as all eyes went to me. My gaze went to Bethany. "Oh, yeah. I pulled some stitches. I'm fine. I was heading to the infirmary next."

"You shouldn't be walking around at all!" Bethany grabbed my arm, ready to pull me away until her eyes caught sight of the two before me. Her mouth gaped and I swear she was drooling a little bit at the two of them.

I bumped her with the arm she was holding. "Put your tongue back in your mouth, Bethany." I switched my attention back to Azeryth and frowned. "So, is this who you were sneaking around to see before?"

Azeryth blushed. An incubus actually blushed. "Yeah. It was."

"And you?" I arched my brow at Jerrod. "How long has this been going on?"

"What?" Jerrod wiped his hand with a cloth and tossed it on his bed, adjusting his own pants. "You think you're the only one allowed to dally with the enemy so to speak?"

I flinched. Just how many people knew about Xavier and me? And here I thought we were being so careful.

At my side, Bethany had finally gotten over her shock and sighed dejectedly. "Ugh man, all the hot guys are always taken."

The incubus's eyes skimmed over her form, purring before licking his lips, "Why don't you join us next time then?"

"Uh...what?" Bethany's eyes widened and she actually took a step back. My sex-crazed roommate was actually surprised by the invitation. I almost laughed out loud. I couldn't imagine how she would have reacted back at Lilith's Touch. She might have an actual heart attack.

"You came here for something, didn't you?" Jerrod interrupted though not showing any jealousy at Azeryth's proposition.

"Yes, I did," I grimaced as I shifted in place. "I need you to go to my room and hang out with Ines."

Jerrod's brows furrowed. "What? Why? She's a big girl, she can take care of herself."

"She needs help dealing with a gift I received from my brother" I gave Jerrod a warning look, before shooting a look at Azeryth and Bethany. Neither of them needed to know what was going on with Michael. Azeryth, because I didn't quite trust him and Bethany because well...I didn't want to traumatize my friend.

Jerrod didn't visibly show he understood what I meant but there was understanding in his eyes that let me know I could trust him to handle it. He inclined his head before turning to Azeryth. He leaned in and kissed the incubus on the cheek. "I'll see you later. Duty calls."

Azeryth stared after him with a look in his eyes I'd only seen between Ines and my brother. Hmmm...good for them.

Bethany moved out of the doorway so that Jerrod could pass. He stopped next to her and whispered something I couldn't hear. Whatever it was made Bethany's face turn beet red and a breathy laugh came out.

Jerrod brushed a strand of blonde hair behind Bethany's ear, letting his finger linger against her face. His face went blank before he walked away.

I stared after him for a long moment until my vision became blurry. Bethany said something to me I didn't understand. My head shifted in her direction almost in slow motion while I asked, "What did you say?"

The world tilted on its axis while Bethany's mouth kept moving but I didn't understand a word she said. Hands I didn't recognize grabbed a hold of me and I was sinking under.

Crap. Guess, I ran out of time after all.

CHAPTER 14

METAL CLINKED NEAR MY head as consciousness came back to me. A humming of low voices buzzed in my ears drawing my attention away from the blissfulness of the dark and back into the harsh light of reality. And the overhead lights of the infirmary were definitely harsh.

"You mean, you're not human? None of you?" Bethany's voice broke through everyone else's. Of course, it would be her that woke me.

I inched up to my elbows, grimacing at the pain in my side. Bethany stood with Azeryth a few feet away from the bed I laid on. Quinn worked next to me cleaning up the bloodied bandages.

"So, you're like some kind of sex demon?" Bethany questioned, not noticing that I'd woken.

Azeryth's lips curved into a lecherous grin, and he closed the distance between them. His hand reached out to brush the air just above her skin and a visible shudder went through her. "Would you like to find out?"

"Ah, miss. You're awake," Quinn interrupted before Bethany could answer. I grunted, watching Azeryth carefully. I wouldn't let any of them take advantage of my friend.

"Yes, just barely." I kept my gaze on Bethany and the incubus. "Thank you."

"Crysta!" Bethany cried out rushing at me. She slapped my arm in rapid succession all the while screeching. "How long have we been friends? And I had to find out I'm not the weirdo friend from someone else?"

"Hey," I lifted my arm up to block her weak and yet stinging attacks. "I'm still injured here."

Bethany growled and slapped my arm one more time. "And you sat there watching all those vampire shows with me probably laughing at me the whole time." Liquid filled at the corners of her eyes as she weakly smacked at me.

My expression softened as I lowered my arm to wrap both around her. Drawing her into a hug, I patted her back while she cried. "Don't worry, Bethany. I've always been the weird one. Nothing's changed there."

Bethany snorted into my shoulder muttering, "Yeah right."

"And I liked those shows. I wasn't laughing at you at all." I pulled back from her and brushed the tears from her cheek with my thumbs. "I enjoyed my time with you."

My friend sniffed and rubbed her nose. "I did too. Though, now I wish I'd pressed you more for information." Bethany locked her firm gaze on me. "Your secrets are zipped up tighter than a nun's vagina."

Azeryth made a choking sound before bursting out laughing. His hands grasping his stomach and bending at the waist. I arched my brow as he collapsed on the floor, still chortling like a hyena.

"It wasn't that funny," Bethany sniffed, leaning into me. "So, what kind of monster are you?"

"Huh?" I pushed against her so I could throw my legs over the side of the bed. "What do you mean?"

"Please don't overdo it this time, miss." Quinn gave me a stern look waving a finger at me. "I don't want to be responsible for the death of our only heir. Abraham would have my neck."

I shrugged sheepishly. "I'll try my best."

Bethany prodded my mouth and then lifted my hair to pull on my ears.

"Ouch, what are you doing?" I jerked away from her poking fingers.

"Looking for fangs or pointed ears...something."

I scowled and pushed her hands away. "I'm as much of a human as you are just, with some improvements."

Bethany glanced me over and sagged almost in disappointment. "Oh, well that's just lame. What kind of monster just looks like a regular old human?"

Azeryth saddled up next to her, slipping a finger down her arm. Some of the residue of his powers slithered over me, making my nipples pebble and thighs clench together. Bethany gasped and moved closer to Azeryth her eyes glazing over from his powers.

"The monsters without claws or fangs are the ones to fear the most." Azeryth purred, his lips inches away from Bethany's lips.

I grabbed his hand and broke his concentration. "That's enough, Azeryth. I think she gets the point."

Bethany blinked. Clarity came back into her vision and a sense of fear came over her face. Suddenly, Azeryth wasn't so appealing anymore.

Azeryth licked his lips and smirked. "Tasty."

Swallowing hard, Bethany let out a shaky laugh. "Uh, yeah. Thanks." Clutching onto my arm, Bethany asked, "Can we go home now?"

"Um...Beth," I pried her off my arm and shifted off the bed so I could stand. "I'm not going home. Or back to the dorm...ever."

Bethany blinked at me. Then jumped to her own feet, grabbing me by the shoulders. "But what about...what about your dream? Your dream to become a doctor? Are you just going to give that all up for this...this...whatever this is?"

"A doctor?" Azeryth arched a brow smirking.

I ignored him and focused on Bethany. "It was never really a dream. More of a way to pass the time." Even as the lie passed through my lips it stung my heart. A part of me wanted to be a doctor. To be a normal human being who could save lives without risking their own. Sadly, that wasn't in the cards for me.

"And this?" she waved her hands around her, her eyes landing on Azeryth for a brief moment before going back to me. "This is what you want to do for the rest of your life? How long do you live anyway?"

I shrugged. "I don't know. Until someone kills me, I guess."

"And you?" she pointed at Azeryth. "Do you live forever?"

Azeryth scoffed a laugh. "Fuck no. Who would want to?" He shot me a look and I had the urge to flip the incubus off. "I have a slightly longer lifespan than humans given by feeding off of sexual energy."

Bethany cocked her head to the side. "How old are you?"

"Younger than grandma over there." Azeryth flicked a finger in my direction.

I could see the wheels turning in Bethany's head before she even opened her mouth, I grabbed her arm and ushered her away from Azeryth. "Time to go. No need to talk about meaningless stuff. Things to do. People to rescue and all that."

"That's right, don't talk about a lady's age, my bad." Azeryth laughed after us.

I shot back. "Don't you have a strip club to get back to?"

Bethany stumbled after me thankfully dropping the subject. "So, where are we going?"

"Uh..." I paused outside the infirmary. "Good question." I let her go and turned to her. "I have to go talk to my father." Bethany opened her mouth. "No, you can't come. My father would blow a gasket if he knew you were here, if he doesn't already."

I dragged a hand over my face and sighed. I wouldn't be surprised if he did know everything already. The bastard tended to have all the answers and not give a shit about any of it. Not the stuff that mattered anyway.

"What do you propose I do then?" Bethany placed her hands on her hips, cocking them to one side. "Just twiddle my thumbs until you get back. I don't think so."

I twisted my lips to one side. "Well, I can't bring you with me."

"She can come with me." Azeryth appeared at the infirmary door. "I was going to pop into the kitchens before heading back." He turned his flirty gaze onto Bethany. "What do you say? Feeling a bit peckish?"

Bethany eyed the hand he offered her warily.

"No powers, I promise." Azeryth held his hand up briefly before offering it once more.

Locking eyes with me, Bethany seemed to be asking me what I thought she should do. I lifted a shoulder and dropped it. "You'll be safe in the kitchens. Whether or not Azeryth will keep his word..." I zeroed in on the incubus with a glare. "He'd better."

Bethany nodded. Ignoring his offered hand, Bethany stepped up to him. "Well then, let's go."

Azeryth smiled a tiny smile and led her toward the direction of the kitchens.

I watched their backs until they went around a corner. I wasn't a hundred percent sure it was a good idea to let Bethany go off with the incubus. However, Azeryth hadn't done anything too bad to her yet. In fact, he seemed just as intrigued by her as Bethany was with him.

Either way, I had my own problems to deal with.

The trek to my father's office was, for once, an uneventful one. The door opened before I could knock, and Eric left the room. His face, usually happy-go-lucky on the worst of days, was clouded over with anger. The moment he realized I was there his expression instantly changed.

"Oh, hey Crysta, didn't see you there," he smiled sheepishly at me. "Don't mind me. Just trying to get some time off so I can go see this concert this weekend."

I frowned. "You go to human functions?"

"Oh yeah." He scratched the back of his head and ducked his gaze. "Don't make fun of me but I love K-pop."

"K-pop?" My brows raised. "Like the boy bands?"

"Hey, don't knock it until you try it. Those guys can really dance and sing! Not to forget, they had to learn a whole other language so the rest of us could enjoy their music too."

I held my hands up before me. "No offense meant. Anyway, I have to get in there. Excuse me." I pushed past him and into the still slightly opened door. I didn't bother knocking this time.

"Ah, you're alive," my father announced the moment I stepped in the room. "I was worried there for a moment if I would lose you too."

The expressionless look on his face didn't match his words.

Stepping closer to his desk, I ignored his jabs and pointed at the small box to the left of him. "I see you received a gift as well."

Father placed his hand on the box and pushed it away. "We will get to that. First, business must be discussed."

My fingers curled into fists and my knees locked. "Your son's mutilated body isn't more important?"

"I did not say that. Do not put words in my mouth, Crysta." My father gestured before him, the first signs of wear showing around his eyes. "Please sit down. We have much to discuss and little time to do so."

Pressing my lips into a thin line, I stiffly sat in the chair behind me. "Fine. Go on. Tell me what's more important than my brother."

He laced his fingers before him and stared over the knuckles. "Your injury at Lilith's Touch was too public. Several people witnessed it and it will be reported back to whoever they belong to. Not to mention the fact that you took home the incubus prince. If you were doing it to strengthen your ties to the succubus queen, then I would applaud your efforts. However, since it was not so and merely to make sure the attackers weren't after him alone, it has put us in quite a predicament."

"What predicament is that?" I frowned. "Just tell them the truth. Someone shot at us, and we don't know who the target was. Case closed."

"That would be the case if the bullets used were not of the normal variety." He opened his side drawer and pulled a small object out of the drawer, placing it on the desk.

"So? They could have still been trying to kill Azeryth and not me. They don't know my weakness. For all we know they were just trying to send a message." My fingers itched to touch the bullet that had been inside of me. What a curious feeling?

Abraham gestured to the bullet with a tug of his lips. "If it was to kill either one of you it would have been a silver bullet or nothing. Even a non-Van Helsing silver bullet would kill an incubus as easily as a human. However, since the attacker didn't bother to use silver at all, it proves that someone knows of your...affliction."

I jerked to my feet. "No, it doesn't." I slammed my hands down on his desk, locking a glare with his impassive gaze. "All it proves is that someone was the target. You can't just make the narrative whatever you want."

My father chuckled, smirking over his hands. "Haven't you learned yet, daughter? That's the power of being the Van Helsing leader. You can make the truth whatever you want, and no one will question it because we are the law."

My jaw dropped, my hands shaking. I couldn't believe the words that had just come out of my father's mouth. Was he implying that he...that we...were the say all to everything? No, he couldn't be. Gritting my teeth, I narrowed my eyes on him. "We're not gods. The moment we start playing at gods is the moment we should step down."

He shook his head slowly and clucked his tongue. "Elise was right. You are still so young. Everyone knows the political game we play is a farce to give the supernaturals some sense of power. They all know that we could crush them in an instant. They live simply by our wills."

I snorted. "Then I guess that means if they all die then there's no use for us anymore. So, who really needs who here?"

His lips curled down for a brief moment caught by my logic. Then he shook his head.

"We shall agree to disagree I suppose. In any case, we are postponing the meeting with the vampires until next week. To give you enough time to recuperate. Unfortunately, we cannot do the same with the shifters with the full moon next week. So we will have a quick and uneventful," he gave me a pointed look before continuing, "visit in three days."

I leaned back from his desk, dropping my arms to my sides. "And what have you told them was the reason why?"

"The shifters don't need a reason, they aren't as calculating as the others. They are after all, animals." he sneered with his words before glancing back at me. "And I figured you could tell Xavier yourself since you are so close with him." Amusement danced in his eyes. "You did mean to meet with him sometime, didn't you? After you promised to cut him off."

My spine stiffened. I hadn't actually. I had no intentions of meeting with Xavier again. I didn't want to break things off with him. Every time I had before it didn't bother me. I never cared. Perhaps because I knew it wasn't forever. This time it would be. And it made something in my chest squeeze tight.

"Yes, of course," my words were rigid.

"Then," he marked something off on a paper next to him as if I were on his to-do list and he was ticking things off. "On to the topic of these little boxes." He turned an unsavory look on the box beside him.

"Have you opened it?"

My father's shoulders tightened, the first sign that the box bothered him. "Of course. I have seen worse."

I stepped forward, my hand automatically reaching for the box. He didn't stop me this time, allowing me to grasp it in my hand and open the lid. This one was much smaller than my own box. Barely bigger than my palm. Inside was a slightly less gruesome sight than my own.

An ear. A single ear with a black stud gleaming in the light.

"They sent a note with it," my father continued, lifting up a wrinkled piece of paper. "Michael was disappointed to hear you weren't looking for him. So, I remedied it." He snorted and leaned back in his chair. "I suppose they think they're being cute."

"I received a box," I murmured, lifting my gaze from the piece of flesh before me. "In my room. A short time ago."

"Who knows about it?" he asked as if talking about the weather.

I swallowed and closed my eyes briefly. "Ines and Jerrod."

"Good. Keep it that way." He glanced off to the side. "We don't need another embarrassment as with the first one."

My eyes locked onto his face, my teeth clenching together tightly. "You're not going to ask what piece of your son I have in a shoe box? What words on the paper they sent me? Do you have any heart at all?" Angry tears burned my eyes.

"Get a hold of yourself." My father barked in return. "Do not say things you do not know anything about. Your brother knew the consequences of being a Van Helsing. He knew what he was getting into as did the rest of the people in this manor. As should you, Crysta."

I sniffed and lifted my chin. "I highly doubt any of them expected to become shish kabob in some sickos game of revenge."

"How do you know it's revenge?"

"Well," I paused, pressing my lips together before continuing, "I don't. Why else would someone go to this extent to torture not only us but Michael? To take him a part piece by piece and send these stupid notes if not to make sure we feel as much pain as they do?"

Father was quiet, his thoughts moving behind his eyes.

"Is there anyone like that?" I pressed him. "Who have you hurt with your god complex to this extent? Why are we being punished for it?"

Huffing a laugh, he shook his head. "Don't you think I'd thought of that? There are simply far too many who hold a grudge against our family."

"Against you, you mean."

"Me, the family, same thing."

It wasn't but I didn't correct him.

"Either way, this cannot be ignored any longer." He stared down at the box on the desk. "They are mocking us. They disrespect our power and that cannot go unpunished."

"What are you going to do then?" I prodded, hoping for some way to be of use.

My father's gaze lifted to mine. "You let me worry about that. Don't you have a visitor here today?" he arched a brow and I forced my face not to react. "Shouldn't you be making sure they don't end up as someone's snack instead of worrying about what I'm going to do."

I flipped my hair over my shoulder and crossed my arms, scowling at him. "Bethany can handle herself better than you think and as the heir shouldn't I know what's going on?"

Pushing to his feet, my father placed his hands on his desk and leaned toward me. "You are not the leader yet and until that time you will do as I ask." He sat back down with a look of finality. "And take care not to tear your stitches again. We can't keep postponing the meetings."

I resisted the urge to touch my side and turned on my heel. Why is it every time I speak to him I feel like hitting something? Probably proof that I should have stayed away.

CHAPTER 15

LATER THAT NIGHT AFTER having beaten a punching bag to a bloody pulp, I sat in my room brushing my hair while Bethany grilled me with questions. Thankfully, Jerrod and Ines were nowhere in sight as well as the box. Someone had even cleaned up the mess I'd made. I didn't want to have to explain any of that to Bethany.

"So, you're like a superhero?"

I glanced at her through the mirror. "Not quite. We keep the peace between the supernaturals."

"And there are three kinds?" Bethany held up three fingers and frowned at them. "Wait, do we count you?"

"Not by my father's standards." I mimicked his voice, "We are not a part of the supernatural community we are above them. Otherwise, we cannot do our job correctly."

Bethany made a face. "Man, I never knew how complicated your life was outside of school." She sat in the middle of the bed and criss crossed her legs. "So, what else? Have you gone to college before?"

I nodded. "Yes, but it was a long time ago."

Arching a brow as she eyeballed me, Bethany asked, "How long?"

I chuckled and shook my head. "What's this obsession with my age?"

Bethany shrugged. "I just want to know what kind of person I've been telling all my darkest secrets to. Are you like, so old it doesn't even matter or are you like...my nana's age?" She wrinkled her nose.

Turning from the mirror, I waved my brush at her. "You should know better than to ask a lady's age."

"Ah," Bethany nodded knowingly. "So, you're older than dirt, got it."

I smiled and went back to brushing my hair. I heard Bethany moving around my room, picking up things and putting them back before settling before the balcony windows.

"It makes me kind of lonely."

I paused slightly. "What does?"

"You're my best friend and I'm learning I didn't know anything about you." Her voice grew low and soft. "It makes me wonder if we were ever really friends at all."

"Oh, Beth." I stood up and walked over to her wrapping my arms around her shoulders to hug her tight. "Out of all the years I've been alive not one person has come as close to being my best friend as you."

"Really?" Bethany murmured. "You're not just saying that to make me feel better?"

I leaned back from her and gave her a soft smile. "Really. Even if you are hornier than the succubi." I pulled away from her as she swatted at me, going back to my seat.

"Hey, I'm a young woman with a healthy sexual appetite. Just because you have chosen the life of a nun doesn't mean I have to." She stuck her tongue out at me in the mirror.

I hummed not correcting her.

If we were keeping count, I've had far more lovers than she would have in her lifetime. Of course, I'd live longer than Bethany as well. As long as someone didn't kill me first.

"Hey Crysta?" Bethany turned from the balcony, pointing her finger out the window. "Isn't that the guy from the alley?"

I dropped my brush and rushed to her side. Peering out the other door, down below stood Xavier. Plain as day not even bothering to conceal himself. The arrogant ass.

Opening the doors, I stepped outside and leaned over the railing. "What are you doing here? You want to get yourself killed?"

Xavier smirked in the moonlight and made a motion with his hand. Before I realized what he meant to do, he had jumped. Hopping from one railing to another until he landed before me on the balcony.

For a brief moment, I considered how easy it had been for him to sneak into the grounds and he had just shown he could get into any room of the manor with ease. Could it be Xavier? Was he the one with the grudge?

It was hard to imagine the vampire I'd taken to bed in the last few decades to be so cruel.

"Woah," Bethany breathed, taking in the vampire before her. "That was a neat trick."

Xavier did an exaggerated bow, grasping Bethany's hand in his. "How good to see one of Crysta's friends again." He shot me a look over Bethany's hand. "She rarely lets me out these days."

I lifted my eyes to the ceiling. It was going to be one of those visits. To Bethany I said, "Why don't you head on to bed. This might take a while."

"Oh, will it, love? I didn't think you had such plans for me tonight. I might have fed first." He flashed his fangs and Bethany gasped. "Kept up my energy and all."

Bethany stepped back from Xavier and nodded quickly. "Uh, yeah. Sure. I'll just go to bed. I'll see you tomorrow." She walked stiffly to the door and then paused to ask, "He's a vampire, right?"

I smiled and shook my head at her timing. "Goodnight, Bethany."

Once she was gone, I turned on Xavier and poked him in the chest several times in a row. "What the fuck is your problem? We're supposed to be a secret." Despite the fact that everyone already seems to know about us, he didn't know that.

Xavier caught my hand with the last poke and drew me close. "What if I don't want to be a secret any longer?" He kissed the pulse of my wrist, brushing his fangs along it. My breath hitched. "What if...I want to be exclusive?"

Blinking several times, I withdrew my hand and gave him my back as I went to pick up my brush. A guise to give me time to process what he was saying. "I don't know what's gotten into you, but you couldn't have worse timing."

Xavier threw himself down on my bed and lounged on it like he owned the thing. My gaze trailed over the pale skin of his chest visible through the handful of buttons he'd left undone of his navy-blue silk shirt. He lifted a leg, placing his leather clad knee up.

"Hey, get your shoes off my bed," I tossed a comb at him. "I swear you're worse than a cat. Always around when you're not wanted and never around when you're needed."

Xavier's lips curled into a wicked grin. "A cat, you say. Well, then this pussy would like to be petted."

I couldn't help but laugh at him. "Really? What the hell Xavier? You never show up unannounced and certainly don't come on this strong."

His confident grin wilted a bit. After a moment, he pulled something out of his back pocket and tossed it before him on the bed.

I sat my brush down, never actually getting to use the thing, and stepped toward the bed. Brows furrowed, I picked up the cell phone. The very one I was missing.

"You left that at my place. I was going to give it to you tonight, but your father rescheduled. So, I thought you might need it." There was a strange vulnerability in his expression that made me uncomfortable.

"Oh, thanks." I sat the phone on the side table. "Is that all?"

"In a hurry to get rid of me, pet?"

Arching a brow, I watched as Xavier stared down at his hands. "Why would I be?"

Xavier shrugged his fingers tracing the pattern on the duvet. "Perhaps you are waiting for your incubus prince to arrive."

I stared at him trying to process what he was saying. "Incubus prince? What incubus..." then it clicked. "Oh, you mean Azeryth?"

Xavier shrugged again.

"Why would I be waiting for him?"

"Well, you did not come to our meeting tonight. Then the supernatural network says you two were seen leaving Lilith's Touch together." Xavier lifted his gaze from the bed to watch me. "What else would I think?"

My lips curled at the edges as I rounded the bed to sit next to him. "That you shouldn't listen to idle gossip and not get the entire story."

Xavier sat up bringing us close together. "So, you're not sleeping with the incubus?"

"His name is Azeryth," I pointed out and then snorted. "And not for his lack of trying."

Xavier frowned, so I added, "Though the way he was all over Jerrod before tells me he might not be that serious with his advances."

"Oh," Xavier said quietly, then his brows rose, "Oh, so he and Jerrod are..."

I nodded.

Xavier's form visibly relaxed.

Curious, I bumped him on the shoulder with mine. "Hey, you weren't jealous, were you?"

"What?" Xavier stood from the bed abruptly. "Me? No. Never. Why? Do you want me to be?"

I frowned at him. "It's not like we both haven't had other lovers before."

"Uh, yeah. I know." Xavier rubbed the back of his neck. "It's just with you becoming the heir and all, I thought maybe you were trying to solidify your power base. I mean, I wouldn't blame you. That's what I would have done."

I pushed to my feet, wincing as the movement pulled on my stitches.

"What's wrong?" Xavier moved to my side.

Straightening, I waved him off. "Nothing. I'm fine."

Xavier sighed. "After all this time you still don't trust me."

My head jerked up. "Should I?"

"I'd think after several decades I would warrant your trust. Have I ever given you a reason not to?" Xavier glowered, crossing his arms over his chest.

Knowing this was going to lead to an argument, I weighed the cons of letting him know what happened at the club.

Coming to a decision, I eased my night shirt up to show him the bandage on my side.

"You are hurt." Xavier reached for my injury, and I let him trace the lines of the bandage. "I see," he said after a moment, dropping his hand. "Did you catch who did it?"

I lowered my shirt. "Sadly, no. But they know me well enough to get bullets that would pierce the armor of my corset lining."

Xavier stared at the wound until I lowered my night shirt. "Was it Van Helsing silver?"

The question made me stare hard at him. Why would he ask that?

Xavier smirked. "Don't look at me with such suspicion. I've known your secret from the moment I tasted your delectable blood." He stroked his fingers along the side of my neck, sending a shiver through me before I remembered myself and pulled away.

"Then how do I know you're not responsible for the attack?"

A sneer crawled up Xavier's face. I stepped back but not fast enough to realize the bed was close behind me, making my knees hit the side of it. Xavier used that weakness to pin me to the bed, his hand around my throat as he hissed in my ear, "If I wanted to kill you, pet I've had ample opportunity while my cock and fangs were buried deep inside of you." He shoved away from the bed and turned his back on me, adding on, "I wouldn't have to shoot you."

I couldn't push away the wicked thrill that went through me at his manhandling. Would he always have such an effect on me?

However, Xavier was correct. He could have killed me any of the times we'd been together. I'd even fallen asleep beside him a time or two. Not once had he threatened my life. I couldn't say the same.

"You're right. I'm sorry." I sank down on the edge of the bed and sighed. "With everything that's changed, being made heir, the attack, and trying to find Michael, I've been a bit on edge. Hard to know who to trust these days."

Xavier spun around. "Find Michael? I thought he was dead."

My eyes widened. Fuck. I'd forgotten it wasn't common knowledge that Michael was still alive. Though it should have been. My father should have been raising hell from the beginning not trying to save face.

I dropped my gaze to the floor not wanting to give away more than I had to. "He's not. Not yet anyway."

Xavier knelt before me. "Then why aren't you out looking for him? Why the farce with all the political bullshit?"

Scowling, I gripped the sides of the bed tight with my fists. "Don't you think I want to? But the almighty Abraham will have none of it. He doesn't want to show weakness at this trying time." I mimicked his voice with a scoff. "It's more of a weakness to let them keep him and send taunting messages to us."

I left out the part about the severed parts. I may trust Xavier but there were some secrets we couldn't risk getting out. Whether or not we can survive after being mutilated was one of them. And so far, it seemed Michael was keeping up with all the trauma to his body. I only hoped it would last.

"I'll make some inquiries." Xavier placed his hands on mine. "If he's out there we'll find him. I promise."

The look in his eyes killed me. Had this meant more to him than just sex? I thought it had been the same for both of us. However, the more I thought about ending it the more I realized none of my threats to him had been serious. I could kill him. If I had to. It would destroy a piece of me to do it, but I would if it really came down to it. At that moment though, I'd rather stare down the barrel of my own gun than do what I had to do next.

"Uh oh," Xavier sighed. "You have that look on your face."

I frowned. "What look?"

He reached up and cupped my chin. "That look that says you're dumping me again. Who is it? The incubus? No wait, we already decided he wasn't interested. Someone else then?"

I didn't respond.

The joking grin on his face fell. "Crysta, pet. What is it?"

"We can't see each other anymore." Might as well rip the band aid off now rather than drawing out the hurt later.

"You need a break. I get it." Xavier huffed a laugh. "I would too with everything going on. On top of being injured."

"No," I grabbed his hand in mine and locked eyes. "It's not that. I could give you all the excuse of why. I'm the heir now. There's just too much at risk. My father says so. But really…who were we kidding? This was never a long-time thing anyway, right?" I offered him a weak smile. "It was just something to pass the time."

Xavier stared at me baffled. "You don't really believe that do you?"

I weakly shrugged a shoulder. "I don't know."

"Well…" Xavier rubbed his chin and shook his head, "Fuck. Here I thought I was being romantic and shit trying to give you what all women want and you're wanting to end it all." He stood to his feet angrily pacing the floor. "I'm a right asshole, aren't I?"

I didn't know what to say. I didn't want to make it worse however, watching him fight to understand was more than I could bear.

Finally, I decided to at least soothe some of his bewilderment. "There's no one else." Xavier paused in his pacing to stare at me. "It's not about you." I dragged a hand through my hair and turned from him. "Hell, it's not even about me."

"Got it. Your father. The clan. It's always about the clan." Xavier stomped over to stand in front of me, grabbing me by the shoulders. "When are you going to do something that's solely for you and not for the benefit of the clan? When will you get to be happy?"

My eyes burned with tears. I pushed them back. "Maybe if Michael was here then things would be different. But how it stands now..." I shook my head. "I just don't know how to make it work without causing issues with everyone else."

Xavier focused on something over my head, not speaking for a long moment. Then he stepped back, unbuttoning his shirt as he peered down at me.

"What are you doing?"

That salacious smirk reappeared on his lips. "If I'm going to lose you, I'm going to need to implant every inch of your body in my memory now."

CHAPTER 16

I GAPED AT XAVIER. "What exactly do you think you're going to do? I'm still injured. I'm not pulling my stitches for a final romp."

Xavier cupped the side of my face and leaned forward. Curious, I allowed him to press his lips to mine. I waited for the gnashing of teeth and the fight for dominance. Except this time there wasn't any of that. Xavier caressed my lips with his own, touching every corner of them until his tongue swept out to taste me.

He coaxed my mouth open with a gentleness that I'd never thought he was capable of. All of our times together had been quick fucks, sometimes angry other times less so, but it always was like we were trying to run away from our problems by losing ourselves in each other.

Not this time.

I opened up to him, letting his tongue sweep along my teeth and dive into the crevices of my cheeks. It was as if he really were trying to memorize every inch of my mouth. It made me grateful I'd already brushed my teeth. It would be embarrassing for him to find leftover food particles in between my teeth.

Xavier pulled his mouth away from mine. "What are you thinking?"

I frowned and then decided to be honest. "That I'm glad I brushed my teeth."

He threw his head back and laughed before taking my mouth once more. This time he was a bit more aggressive in his search of my mouth. I found myself pulling away first this time to breathe. Xavier didn't let it deter him.

One moment he was before me the next he had me up and in his arms. I let out a little eep of surprise, clinging to him.

"What do you think you're doing?" I held onto him tightly as he climbed onto the bed.

Xavier grinned. "I think I like you like this, clinging to me like I'm your only hope."

I resisted the urge to roll my eyes at him. "Believe me you're the last person I'd come to for help."

This only made him chuckle and lower me slowly to the bedspread. "Always so quick with that sharp tongue of yours." His lips curled wickedly. "Let's see if we can silence it."

Before I could ask him what exactly he thought he was going to do to quiet me, his mouth found the side of my neck. He didn't pierce my skin like I would normally expect him to do. Instead, he traced his tongue along the line of my pulse making it quicken under his ministrations.

I gasped and my eyes fluttered closed.

In the few odd decades we'd been together, Xavier had somehow made my body automatically heat just from peppering my neck with kisses. It was like it knew what was coming and wanted to be ready for it.

I couldn't exactly complain. Those times usually ended with multiple knee quivering orgasms. However, it made me wonder if anyone else but him touched me there, would I have the same reaction? I hadn't tried it and at that very moment couldn't imagine letting someone else encroach on his territory.

Xavier's mouth moved down my neck and his tongue traced along the neckline of my shirt, dipping between my breasts before coming back up the other side. His hands lifted the bottom of my shirt and I shifted to allow him room to bring it over my head.

Laying back down, I watched him just look at me. He didn't touch me, didn't resume his kissing. Xavier's eyes burned a path across my skin as if he were memorizing every single detail. The intensity of his gaze made me wiggle in place and want to turn the lights off. When I reached for them, he stopped me.

"I want to see you," he said simply and there was something in his voice that made me want to give him what he wanted.

Either he was done looking or he noticed how it was making me uncomfortable because Xavier took one strap of my bra and drew it down, his mouth following in its path. He did the same to the other side until he reached behind me and expertly unclipped my bra. The material sagged on my front and at his prompting I lifted my arms so he could remove it.

This wasn't the first or even the hundredth time I'd been bare chested in front of him and yet this time it was different. My nipples pebbled and my breasts grew heavy, aching to be touched.

Xavier took his time though.

Brushing his thumbs along each side of my breasts, he traced the curve of them avoiding the tips until I was arching into his touch.

"So impatient as always," he murmured with a male satisfaction.

I pursed my lips at him, scowling. "Then hurry up."

"No," he clipped sharply. "I will take my time with you until I can draw out every ounce of pleasure your body can take and perhaps then, I will let you go."

The way he said it shut up every protest from me. It was the last time we'd ever be together. Could I really take this away from him?

I shifted my head to the side of the pillow. "Am I allowed to touch you as well?"

Xavier's lip ticked up. "Of course, you aren't tied down, are you?" The way he said it made me think there was a yet he left unsaid.

Given permission, I sat up and grabbed his shirt, tugging on the remaining buttons until his chest was bare before me. "There," I breathed, tracing the scars on his chest. "We're even now."

"Oh, no, love." Xavier purred, leaning me back once more. "We're not even close."

Taking the tip of my breast into his mouth, Xavier lapped and pulled at it until my knees shook. I grabbed at his hair, pulling at him. Finally, he relented and proceeded to mimic what he had done to my other nipple. When he was done, I could hardly breath and my body ached for release. Something he had promised but had yet to allow me to have.

"Is this your plan?" I asked between breaths. "To make me beg for you?"

Xavier smiled. "I just want you to remember what you will be missing out on. I have to make an impression or what's the point?"

Throwing my head back on the pillow, I gasped out, "I hate you."

"Oh, I know." Xavier chuckled against my abdomen, trailing his torture devices down across my belly button. He paused at my bandage and began to peel the tape back. I stopped him by shifting away. "Let me heal you."

I shook my head. "Don't. If I heal so suddenly those who knew I was hurt would question what happened."

Staring at me for a long moment, Xavier seemed like he might do it anyway but then thought better of it, leaving my wound to lick at my hip bones just above my panties. My hips jerked each time he nipped at them, and my insides clenched desperately for some kind of friction. Something I knew I wasn't going to get any time soon.

So far, Xavier had kept everything pretty tame, keeping his mouth and hands above the waist. Now that he'd gotten to the lower half, I wasn't letting my hopes rise at the prospect of getting what I wanted.

To my surprise, Xavier fingered my panties and slowly slipped them down my hips. I eagerly assisted him hoping he was moving this along already. Sadly, Xavier didn't bury his face between my thighs like I wanted. Instead, he lifted one of my legs and began to lavish it with attention, bypassing my quivering center completely. He laid my ankle on his shoulder, spreading my thighs wide so he could see the proof of my need.

"Now that's a sight I'll never forget," he murmured against my knee, sliding his tongue along the backside of it before scraping his fangs along the same area. I'd never found my knees sexy and yet it made them feel utterly that way. Each touch of his mouth was a straight shot to core, and I couldn't help but let out a lengthy moan.

"Had enough?" He chuckled darkly.

"Yes," I groaned, spreading my legs wider to tempt him to stop torturing me.

Flashing his fangs at me, Xavier moved further down my leg. "Too bad."

When his mouth found the bottom of my foot, I hissed out, "Fuck." Why did that feel so good? I was so worked up that a hot poker through my chest would probably feel just as good, but damn did I want him to do that again.

To my dismay, Xavier left my foot and started at the beginning of my other leg, this time pausing to press his face close to my wetness. "Gods above, I'll miss this scent."

I'd have been embarrassed had I not wanted him to bury his face in me right then. I bucked my hips up trying to get some kind of friction from him. He rewarded me with a lap of his tongue right on my clit before moving away.

"No," I cried out and reached for him. "Come on already. You want me to beg? Fine. I'll beg." I locked eyes with him, cupping my breasts so they pressed together and moaned out, "Please Xavier, fuck me now."

Xavier's mouth dropped open slightly, pausing with my leg in his hand. Thinking I almost had him, I moved my hands down my stomach and spread my lips open for him, circling a finger around my own clit. "I'm going to explode if I don't have you inside of me right now."

Clicking his tongue, Xavier shook his head slowly from side to side. "Now that's not playing fair, pet." His hands went to the belt on his pants, and he unclipped it, removing it at a glacial pace.

Thinking he was going to give me what I wanted, I licked my lips and reached for his pants. Xavier snatched my hands up with his own. I frowned and then tried to jerk my hands away when he clasped them both together, wrapping his belt around them and cinching it tight. Using the left-over length, he dragged my hands up and over my head, tying it off on the headboard.

"You're a fucking asshole, you know that?" I scowled, tugging on the belt for good measure. It was good quality leather and with an extra push of strength I could probably break it...Xavier distracted me from my escape plans by holding my legs out wide and blowing on my center. The cool air from his mouth against my hotness made me struggle against my binds, bucking my hips up for more.

"Now, now, kitten. Be a good girl and I'll give you what you want." At his words, I stopped fighting my restraints immediately. Out of the two of us, Xavier was by far the more patient and also the best at fulfilling his promises and then some.

Forcing myself to calm down, I lifted my head to watch him. Xavier focused on the spot between my legs, not touching it just admiring it.

Growling with frustration, I asked, "Are you just gonna stare at it all day?"

Lips ticking up, Xavier pondered, "Have I ever told you how you have the prettiest pussy I've ever seen?"

I snorted. "I highly doubt that. You're like three hundred. I'm sure there are plenty of others who's better than mine."

"That's just it," Xavier continued, talking to it. "I've had all manner of man, woman, and beast and nothing comes close to the gorgeous sight of your pink flesh all wet and warm for me. If someone killed me today, I'd be a happy man knowing I'd tasted such a perfect pussy."

I couldn't help but laugh. "Are you serenading it? I can assure you, I'm good and ready to go."

"Shhh," Xavier stroked a finger down the length of me and my words caught in my throat. "We're having a moment."

I clamped my mouth shut in hopes that he wouldn't stop.

Those nimble fingers slid along each side, touching every inch of the outside of me until I was shaking with need. The only place he hadn't paid much attention to stood at attention and felt like a thousand heart pulses were beating through it, crying out to be touched.

"You do make the more delectable sounds," Xavier said finally before lavishing my clit with attention. Each stroke of his tongue made my hip buck and a choking gasp to escape my lips. He pulled it into his mouth careful of his fangs to suck until my vision went hazy. I buried my face into the side of my arm trying to muffle my screams.

There was one big glaring negative about living in a house with your entire clan. Everyone and I do mean everyone could hear your exploits if you weren't careful. The last thing I needed was for one of them to come rushing in and find me tied to the bed with the Master Vampire between my legs. Not only would it implicated things against him but it would be mortifying as fuck.

"Quiet, love." Xavier spoke against me. "Or you'll have the whole house down on us."

I glared at him.

Not moved by my look, Xavier continued his work, moving that talented tongue of his down to dip inside of me. Thrusting the hot muscle several times inside of me, he gave me just enough to move to that edge once more before slithering out and tracing the line to my asshole.

There were many things Xavier and I have explored together anal being one, but I had a feeling he didn't want me there tonight.

Proving me right, Xavier slid his tongue across it briefly before coming back to my front. With a wistful sigh, Xavier pulled back. "I am going to miss that ass of yours. You squeal so nicely when I fuck you with both my fingers and cock."

I wiggled in place at his words, remembering how good it had felt, how full. A part of me wished we'd do it now and yet I was at Xavier's mercy. I was after all, the one breaking things off.

Why was I doing that again? Seemed like a stupid idea now...

"Did I lose you, pet?" Xavier asked, cocking his head to the side. My eyes locked back on his and then the movement of his arm. When had he removed his pants? I must have really been spacing out.

"Uh...sorry." I muttered, my eyes on his hand wrapped around his hard cock.

"I must not be doing my job right if you're drifting on me." Xavier jerked his hand up and down his length, drawing my attention to the liquid beading up at the tip. My tongue swiped across my lip on its own, wanting nothing more than to taste him in return. Xavier, however, had other ideas.

Lowering himself between my thighs, Xavier moved the tip of him up and down my slit, stopping to circle around my clit every few strokes. My eyes squeezed closed to focus on the sensation.

"Open your eyes," Xavier demanded between heavy breaths. "I want you to remember who it is touching you. So that when you're fucking someone else, you'll remember that none of them will be as good as this..." he pushed himself inside of me until he couldn't go any further and we both groaned at finally getting what we both so desperately needed.

We rarely looked at each other while we did this. Or at least, I didn't. I usually looked off somewhere else or closed them focusing on the feeling and trying to forget whatever it was I was running from. I couldn't say the same for Xavier. Has he always been looking at me? The thought made something in my chest tighten.

The sound of our flesh slapping against one another filled my ears. I tried to wrap my legs around Xavier to control the movements, but he wouldn't let me. He held my legs up and pulled back just slightly so he could watch himself slide in and out of me, alternating with watching my face.

I had to admit the sight made it all the better. I could watch his reactions too. Could see how his eyes dilated when he felt something particularly good. How when he was focusing, he pressed his lips tightly against his fangs almost piercing them. How had I missed this? I suddenly felt like a total ass hole using him all this time when he clearly knew me better than I knew myself.

"Don't look at me like that, Crysta," Xavier commanded, pushing into me this time at a more punishing pace. "We used each other. I could have walked away at any time."

"Let me go," I told him, tugging on my binds. Part of me realized that those words were a plea for something else as well. I shoved that thought to the back. Xavier freed my hands, and I found my hands moving up and around his neck, pulling him toward me. Our mouths collided in an almost desperate kiss, each of us clinging to the other as our hips dragged out our pleasure.

When I orgasmed, it was almost bittersweet. A part of me wanted to freeze us in this moment of time and never look outside my bedroom door. It was a childish thought and as Xavier dressed, I clung to my pillow as if it could somehow keep me from reaching out to him.

"I guess this is it," Xavier said finally. I kept my eyes on the wall opposite of him not able to meet his gaze. "I'll just let myself out then." He stepped toward me and then seemed to think better of it. It wasn't until he had been gone a long time that I finally crawled out of the bed and went to the shower.

I stood under the spray ignoring the blood from my injury that had pulled open a little bit. I welcomed the pain. It reminded me I wasn't dead inside. Even if I felt it.

CHAPTER 17

THE GODS MUST BE watching over me. Three days and not a single incident. No ugly red boxes. No random attacks. Just three days of healing and... Bethany.

I love my best friend, but she was driving me crazy with her questions. So, when the day finally came to resume my visits with the shifters it was also time for Bethany to go.

"But Crysta! I don't wanna go," Bethany whined at the doorway of the manor. "I've never seen a shifter before. I saw an incubus and a vampire, it's only fair I get to see a shifter too."

Placing my hand on her shoulders, I shook my head. "It's much too dangerous. You're a human. There's no telling how they would react if I brought you along. Also, you've already missed enough class. Do you want to get kicked out?"

Bethany puffed up her cheeks and then retorted, "Like you're one to talk."

I sighed, dropping my arms. "I'm sure my father has already taken care of withdrawing me from school so there's no use arguing. Besides, the shifters aren't like the others. Right, Jerrod." I caught my cousin's eye on the way by. "Tell Bethany all about the shifters."

Jerrod paused in his tracks, twisting our way. "Oh, no. Don't get me involved. I have enough women riding my ass already. I don't need another one."

Bethany snorted and muttered, "Not the only thing riding your ass."

Jerrod's large shadow appeared over Bethany, his beefy arm bracing against the door over her head as he leaned in. "What was that now?"

Throwing her back against the door, Bethany stared up at Jerrod with a mixture of awe and fear. She seemed to lose her thoughts for a moment and then snapped out of it. Bethany smirked up at him. "You heard me."

"Jealous?" Jerrod purred, wrapping her blonde hair around one of his fingers. "Perhaps, you'd like to ride me instead?"

I cleared my throat. "Okay, that's enough mental scarring for today." I grabbed Jerrod by the back of the shirt and pulled him away from Bethany. Jerrod scowled at me so I added, "I'll give her your number and you two can boink to your heart's content...as long as it's away from me."

Bethany flushed, giggling into her hand before giving Jerrod one more sideways look. "You better call me."

Jerrod chucked his finger under her chin. "You can count on it."

"Yeah, yeah. Alright already." I opened the front door and waved an arm out of it. "Get going already. If you go now, you'll be in time for afternoon classes."

Bethany pouted. "Fine. I'll just go the rest of my life without ever having met a shifter."

Jerrod snorted. "Count yourself lucky. Bunch of mangy animals. Marking their territory, causing fights over stupid things, not to mention the fact that they never stay clothed."

I groaned and smacked my forehead as Bethany's eyes brightened. "Jerrod," I drew out. "Now, I'm never going to get her to leave."

"Oh, come on, Crysta!" Bethany pumped her fists in front of her. "I wanna see the naked shifters."

"Forgotten already," Jerrod chuckled, shaking his head.

"Why don't you let Crysta befriend one first?"

We turned to see Ines standing near the stairs, her eyes narrowed on me an angry kind of aura coming from her.

Ines pushed off the stairs and stalked over to us. "She seems to have a knack for that. Bringing home vampires and succubi."

I studied her for a long moment, trying to figure out what I had done wrong. As far as I knew, Ines didn't have a problem with vampires or succubi. So why was she so mad?

"Oh, don't mind her," Jerrod commented, crossing his arms over his chest. "She's just bitchy because she's the last to know you were screwing that vampire."

Bethany cocked her head to the side. "You didn't know? I just found out about vampires, and I knew she was banging that dude."

I jolted. "You did?"

Rolling her eyes, Bethany patted me on the shoulder. "Oh, babe. You're a lot of things but discrete isn't one of them."

I eye balled her. "I still kept my identity hidden from you for three years."

Bethany shrugged, holding her hands up. "What can I say? When it comes to anything other than the matters of the heart, I'm as oblivious as you. Anyway," she saluted with two fingers and winked at Jerrod. "Check ya later." Turning on her heels, she skipped and called out, "Oh, Gerald! Where is my gorgeous bald man?"

"That girl," I huffed. Then I turned to Ines, waiting for her to get on with it. When she didn't say anything, I ran my fingers through my hair, gathering it up to pull over my shoulder. "Look, I gotta get ready or my father's going to be on my ass. So, if you're going to yell at me, do it while you help me dress." I sniffed and grimaced. "I'm sure he has some kind of ridiculous outfit he wants me to wear tonight so I don't offend their delicate alpha male senses."

"Hey, I resent that," Jerrod pointed out.

I arched my brow. "Which part? Cause last time I checked you still end up on your back when we fight."

"Ouch." A passing trainee called out, laughing with his teenage friends. "She got you good."

Jerrod turned on the adolescents and placed his hands on his hips. "What was that Miles? You want to do a hundred pushups before breakfast all week long?"

The boy, Miles, blanched and shook his head, his laughter gone. "No, no. I didn't say anything, sir. Right guys?" He turned to his friends, but they had all taken off, leaving him to fend for himself. "Oh shit, wait up!" He hurried off before Jerrod could get on to him more.

"Damn brat." Jerrod curled his fingers into a fist and shook it in the air.

I laughed and patted him on the shoulder as I walked by. "You look like an old man yelling at the kids to get off his lawn."

"No, I don't," Jerrod called after me, which Ines answered with, "Yeah, you do," before following after me.

Ines and I walked in silence on the way to my bedroom. There was a tension between us that had rarely been there before. I had a feeling there was more on her mind than just my affair with Xavier.

Expecting her to come after me once we were behind closed doors, I went to my wardrobe and opened it knowing she would do what she willed. Inside my wardrobe sat another disgustingly puffy dress. This time in a soft pink that probably was meant to make me look less threatening.

"Does he really expect you to wear that?" I glanced over my shoulder at Ines, sitting on the bed. She made a face at the dress. "I mean, I get trying to make friends, but does he think that pretending to be some delicate flower after you grabbed the alpha by the balls is really going to work?"

Pulling the dress from the hanger, I held it up with my lips twisting to the side. "It does give off the wrong kind of message, doesn't it?"

Ines stood up and went to the dress, lifting up a piece of the frilly fabric. "If he wants the alphas to listen to you, that's not going to happen if they just see you as a piece of ass. Females aren't that high up in hierarchy anyway. This is just gonna make them put you in the same box."

I frowned at her words. I knew she was right. I just couldn't figure out how to get around wearing it without causing a fight. I already had enough to deal with tonight, I wanted my father on my side for once.

Smirking, I reached down and pulled out the knife latched to my thigh. "I think a bit of a makeover is in order, don't you?"

Ines pulled her own knife out, a wicked grin on her lips. "I have a few ideas."

It took a few minutes, but we finally got the dress into something that I could actually stomach wearing.

Adjusting the bodice so that my cleavage peaked out, I made sure that I could reach all of my weapons through the shredded skirt. I'd kept the hideous bow on the back but paired the dress with knee high boots.

"Looks good," Ines nodded, surveying our handy work. "Now..." Her fist swung out and I barely had time to put my arm up to block it in time. "You're still quick. Good."

I arched a brow. "I didn't just sit on my ass, reading books and going to keggars all the time you know."

Nodding, Ines dropped back into a relaxed stance. "Very well."

I didn't drop my guard yet. "Was that it? Nothing else you want to say?"

Ines turned to the side, her eyes on the door. At first, I thought she wasn't going to say anything else and then she stated, "Don't leave me behind."

"Huh?"

"When you go after them to save Michael, don't leave me behind." She tilted her head to the side, locking her gaze with mine.

"Are you sure you can handle it?"

Closing her eyes briefly, Ines fixed them on the floor. "I can. I know I haven't proved it so far, but you know when it comes down to it, I can get the job done. And for Michael..." she clenched her hands into fists. "I'll do whatever I have to."

I inclined my head. "Understood. Then let's do our best to bring Michael back."

"But first we have some dick wad shifters to deal with." Ines brushed her braids over her shoulder. "Try not to kill anyone tonight."

I smirked, following her to the door. "I can't promise that."

When we reached the foyer, my father was impatiently waiting. My father took one look at my outfit and closed his eyes, sighing. "Let's get this over with."

Ines and I exchanged a grin as we followed him out of the manor. He and I would take the limo and the others, including Ines, would follow after in separate vehicles. We tried to have the meeting here in the manor. In fact, every alpha before had agreed to meet us on our turf rather than us coming to their sacred grounds.

However...this new young big shot alpha seems to have something to prove. He wouldn't budge an inch and demanded we come to him.

"This will be the first time in three hundred years the shifters have allowed the Van Helsings to enter their sacred land," my father commented once we were in the limo together. "Be on your guard. We don't know what they might be planning."

I leaned on my hand, staring out the window. "Can't be worse than sending body parts in a box." Glancing away from the window, I asked, "How is the search going for Michael? Any leads?"

My father's gaze flicked up from the folder in his hands. "There's a task force working on it. They've hunted down a few rogues and are interrogating them. So far there's been nothing to report."

Clenching my jaw, I slammed my fist against the door. "Isn't that what you did when he first disappeared? If it didn't work then, why would it work now?"

"There are procedures that have to be followed," my father snapped, glaring in my direction. "And your childish outbursts will not make things proceed faster."

"Fuck procedure," I raised my voice maybe because he'd just called me childish. "You need to think outside of the box. Whoever has Michael is a sick bastard who shows no mercy. We have to be the same. Scour every possible lead."

"Don't you think I've done that?" My father snarled, clipping his folder shut firmly. "I am at a loss. We hunted down every creature who might have been in the area when your brother went missing. Every member of his team was interrogated until there was blood on the floor. Do not act as if you know everything. You know nothing."

I gnashed my teeth at him. "And who's fault is that? Had you told me when Michael first disappeared then I could have helped. I could have -"

"What?" he asked, suddenly calm. "What could you have done?"

"Huh?" I was taken back by his sudden question. "What do you mean?"

My father crossed his legs and arms, turning toward me. "Tell me, what would you have done differently? You will be the next leader of our clan. I want to know how you will proceed if something like this were to happen again."

"I..." Pausing, I really thought about it. What would I have done differently?

"Well?"

Straightening my back, I lifted my chin. "For one, I wouldn't keep it a secret. One of your problems is that you look down on the supernaturals too much. You don't trust them, and they don't trust you. If that were to change then you would have not only the Van Helsings looking for Michael but all of the houses. Then this might not have happened in the first place."

My father huffed. "You think it's that simple huh?"

I stared at him, not backing off.

"Hmmm. Then I suppose that means you need to make amends with the alpha shifter even more now than ever, yes?" His lips curled up in a self-satisfied smile that irritated me to no end.

Unfortunately, he was right. If I wanted to make my world of trust and honesty a reality, then I had to be the one to start it. I already had Xavier on my side, and it looked as if my saving Azeryth's life had put me in good with the succubi. Now I had to.... for lack of a better word, make friends with the shifters. Damn Ines. She's always fucking right.

CHAPTER 18

THE SHIFTERS WEREN'T LIKE the vampires and succubi. They didn't want to live among the humans pretending to be part of the world. They made their own sanctuary up in the mountains hidden by a dense forest. It made it almost impossible for anyone to simply stumble upon their sacred lands.

Arcadia.

For the most part, the shifters kept to their own community. Out of all the supernaturals we had fewer human-shifters issues. Most of their problems revolved around infighting. However, every once in a while, some of the shifters would get antsy.

They would get tired of living apart from the world and want a taste of what the human world was like. Which would be fine if they could keep their tempers and not go on a rampage every time their feelings were hurt.

Bunch of crybabies.

"When we get there," my father began as we began to ascend the mountain on foot. We couldn't get there by car. It would make it too easy for the humans to find it. "I suggest you find a way to curb that tongue of yours. We do not want to start a fight while we are in their territory and are outnumbered."

I frowned as I stepped over a pile of rocks. "I thought we were only meeting the alpha and his close circle?"

My father shook his head, ducking under a tree branch. "We may only be meeting with the alpha, however the rest of the shifter community will be just a few yards away. All he would have to do is give the signal and they would fall upon us like ravaging wolves. No pun intended."

It had been a while since I'd studied up on the supernatural's home bases. The vampires and succubi were easy. They thrived around humans and wanted nothing more than to pretend they were them, even going so far as to live separately in their own homes. The shifters didn't have that same kind of mentality. They wanted to be close to the pack and only the pack mattered.

The shifters were not like regular animals. In the wild, lions, tigers, wolves and even bears would not be found living in harmony together. There would be too much fighting for dominance, trying to kill off the other species. I suppose that's one of the major things that set the shifters apart from their counterparts.

"A werewolf is in charge now, right?" I asked my father for confirmation. "That Joe guy."

"Yes," he answered, checking the surrounding areas for a moment before continuing on. It had been hundreds of years since he'd come to the mountains, I wondered if he still knew the way. "The last alpha was a weretiger."

I frowned and stared down at the ground as I walked. "How does that work exactly? I know they all live together and it works but how does it work? Shouldn't they be fighting all the time like the animals would?"

My father laughed as did several other Van Helsing following after us. It was Jerrod who answered my question, "You really have been away too long. The shifters are broken up into factions. Each type of shifter has their own community within the whole. Those factions have their own leader, I guess you could call it."

I was getting it. "And all the factions answer to Joe."

"Right," Jerrod inclined his head. "And the only way they get a new leader is if the old leader dies."

Joe must have killed the last leader so he could be in charge. It made sense in a way. Though something still bugged me.

"What if their leader is a bad guy?" I wondered aloud. "What if they're a tyrant that is just making their lives miserable and no one can defeat them. What do they do then?"

My father answered this time. "That, my dear, is where we come in."

We walked for about an hour before we finally began to see a bit of separation in the trees. There were signs of life here outside of the normal animals and hikers. A line of clothing here. A few shacks that seemed to be used for storage. What really told us that we were there was a large stone archway carved in the same of all the were's animal parts with the middle marking a large 'A'.

I didn't really know what I expected. Maybe a bunch of tents set up around a large fire pit? What I didn't expect to see was a town in the middle of the forest.

Once we stepped through the stone archway, our feet moved from dirt and grass to stone and gravel. Shops lined the walkway, everything from grocers to clothing stores. They even had a center square with a fountain. The fountain statue had one of each kind of were; lion, tiger, bear, and wolf, all standing together. Each animal pointed in one direction of the walkway leading down a road of humble sized houses.

There were a few shifters wandering about going in and out of the buildings. They stopped when they noticed us and sniffed the air. Whatever they smelled made them back away from us and before we knew it, we were alone on the street.

"Warm bunch aren't they," someone muttered behind me.

"I didn't realize they had..." I tried to figure out a way to say it without sounding like an ass. "Electricity and such."

Ines chuckled beside me, having caught up. "I forgot you haven't been here before. Anyone over three hundred has been here, though they have improved a lot since we've come last." Ines peered around the area just as interested as me.

"I wonder how they power the town?" I commented more to myself than to anyone else. Though someone answered.

"Light panels and turbines." We all turned to the voice of the new alpha approaching us. He wore a shirt though he left it unbuttoned so the dark planes of his muscles were visible between the flaps. At least this time he was wearing pants and shoes. I couldn't imagine trying to have a serious talk while he was naked.

Unaware of my thoughts, Joe stared at me and added on, "We aren't barbarians. We even have running water." He gave me a long arrogant look. He was trying to embarrass me, and I wouldn't play his game. My father might think I had to play nice to make friends with the alpha, but I'd already learned that being meek and quiet wouldn't get me anywhere with this shifter.

"Alpha Joe," my father greeted, offering his arm for the alpha to shake. "It is an honor to visit Arcadia once again. I do have to say, you have done wonders since I was here last."

Joe clasped my father's forearm with his hand, and they shook. "Well, I can't take all the credit. I was still a pup when they finally put the electricity in."

My father chuckled. "It's still a far cry from those wagons and tents that used to be all bunched together around the area."

Shrugging, Joe didn't take offense. "Sometimes I think we might have done better staying that way." His dark gaze went to the sky where he squinted up at the sun as he murmured, "We spend too much time indoors and not enough out with nature."

"I can understand that." My father continued as Joe began to lead us toward the large main building on the other side of the square. "No matter how long I live, I cannot understand the world today. They'd rather fiddle with their electronic devices than enjoy the world around them."

I trailed after them as they spoke about the old days and such, very much being ignored by both of them after the first initial encounter. The asshole hadn't even bothered to greet me. Not that my father had tried to remedy it with a reintroduction.

"Your face is doing that thing again," Ines murmured at my elbow.

"What thing?" I asked, staring after the two of them as chummy as ever.

"Where it says you're contemplating murder and don't care who knows about it."

I sniffed and smiled slightly. "Maybe I am."

Ines shook her head. "Then perhaps you should hide it better lest your enemies expect it."

I wrinkled my nose at her before moving up closer to my father and Joe. Ines fell back with the other Van Helsings. Joe threw open the two large double doors and ushered us all inside. I half expected the alphas home to be over the top extravagant the way that he portrayed himself as better than all of us. The building wasn't really a house at all, more of a meeting place with chairs lined along the sides and a large empty area in the middle. At the front had a little dais and four chairs behind a table.

"The meeting hall has greatly changed," My father commented, looking around. "I remember when it was just a pile of stone in a field."

Joe snorted. "Yeah, well, what can I say, our ancestors liked being able to see the sky all the time." He shrugged as if it weren't a big deal and moved to the front of the room. Once we were all inside, other doors opened, and shifters poured in around us.

"What is the meaning of this?" My father commanded, his hand going for the blade at his side.

My eyes scanned the shifters as I flicked the clasp on both my holsters but didn't draw them. At first it seemed as if we were being ambushed. Then a closer look showed that not all the shifters were in fighting health. Some elderly came ambling up the room, being helped into seats along the wall as well as the pregnant and disabled. Those who were not in need of a chair gathered around us, though, keeping their distance.

"Come now, Abraham." Joe chuckled, crossing his arms over his large chest. "Do you really think I brought you here to attack you?" His gaze dipped to me and grunted. "We may be part animal, but we don't kill each other for offenses from the young."

I scowled up at him. "If someone had kept their hands to themselves then the young wouldn't have to reciprocate."

"She's so mouthy," Joe spoke to my father as if I didn't exist. "How do you keep her from getting her throat ripped out? I hardly think the vampires have half the patience it takes to deal with her."

Jerrod and Ines made a choking sound like they were trying to stifle their laughter.

My father ignored them and simply stated, "She has her mother's spirit and yet I find myself growing weary of it."

Joe nodded as if that explained everything. "Now then," he turned to the whole room. "We have all gathered here for the first meeting in three centuries, the Van Helsings and the shifters. We shifters have long since governed ourselves without the help of the Van Helsings, hence the reasoning for the lack of invitation to Arcadia." He paused for a moment so that everyone could comprehend his words. "Now, times have changed. We cannot stay hidden in the forest while the world moves on around us. We have many who would like to be more involved with the humans and we need to know that the Van Helsing will be able to do their job and keep the peace." His lips curled up slightly on one side. "We of course cannot be everywhere at once and if we encroach on the territory of the others there will surely be war."

There were a few mutters from the crowd. However, for the most part they let Joe speak. Perhaps he was not such a hot-headed leader as his first appearance had led me to believe.

My phone buzzed in my boot. I ignored it until it stopped.

"I can assure you that the Van Helsings are fully capable of keeping the peace," my father answered loudly for all to hear. "We have done so for the last five hundred years and will do so for the next."

My phone vibrated again. Still, I ignored it.

Joe stared at my father. "That is true. But during that time, you were in charge Abraham. Isn't it my understanding that you are retiring? Won't your daughter be taking your place," Joe looked at me as if I were a piece of gum on his shoe. "How do we know your daughter will be able to handle the responsibility? That she will be able to deal with the problems as they need to be dealt with?"

Two short buzzes. Fuck already. I grabbed my phone. If the asshole was gonna talk shit about me right to my face, then he didn't deserve my attention.

The alpha continued talking while I glanced down at my phone. Two missed calls from Xavier and one text message. All it said was, "I found him. An old building on Prescot Street."

Words continued in the background as I stared down at the message. Xavier had done it. He had found Michael. I felt a bit guilty since I'd dumped him and yet Xavier still came through for me in the end.

" How am I to - am I boring you?"

My father bumped me, and I glanced up from my phone. He gave me a warning look, jerking his eyes back toward the front.

When I finally turned my attention back to the shifter before me, he asked with a snarl, "I said, Am I boring you?"

Without rushing, I slipped my phone back into my boot and then straightened, locking my eyes on Joe's black ones. "To be honest, yes."

"Crysta!" My father cried out reaching for me as Joe growled, "Why you little-"

I stepped forward and held my hand up. "No more. I have stood here and listened to you not only insult me but our entire clan. You don't trust us to do our job, or I suppose you don't trust me. Is it because I got the best of you or because I'm a woman?"

Joe stood there fuming but didn't interrupt me again.

My father tried to fix things for me. "I apologize for my daughter's insolence. She doesn't quite have the mindset yet for these kinds of gatherings."

"No," I moved in front of him, turning my back on Joe. "You are the ones who want to play 'who has the best poker face' and I'm tired of it."

"You turn your back on me?" Joe asked with a surprised tone. "Either you are very stupid, or you think I am weak which is it?"

Slowly turning from my father, I tilted my head to the side scanning him. "Well, we've already established that you're not a weakling. And some might consider me stupid for my ideologies that is neither here nor there." I shrugged. "What I am going to do is tell you what I told the succubus queen."

"And what was that?"

"I'm trying to shape a new world. I don't know about you, but I don't want to live in theirs anymore." I pointed my thumb back at my father. "You became alpha to make a change, correct? How about you start now?" Joe jerked his head once in response. "I am about honesty and trust. You cannot have one without the other. I will be honest with you right now as a sign of that trust."

Shifting so I could see my people as well as Joe, I raised my voice. "Michael is not dead. Not yet anyway. Someone has kidnapped my brother and has been sending us pieces of him in little boxes." There was an array of gasps and startled words from both the shifters and our own. My father looked ready to murder me and yet I kept going. "I don't know about you but that pisses me off. If I understand correctly, you shifters are all about the pack." I shot a look at Joe and then around the clearing. "The pack comes before anything else. Well, my brother is part of my pack, and I can finally rescue him." I stared at my father for a long moment before I said, "I will not put power games above my family. If another meeting is required, I will be there but I'm leaving now to save my brother." I added silently, since no one else will.

My father gaped at me. For once speechless.

No one stopped me as I walked through the crowded area and back toward the door. Ines and Jerrod moved as soon as I got to them, shifting into place behind me. Then to my surprise several other Van Helsings, including Eric, followed their lead.

Hold on, Michael. I'm coming for you.

CHAPTER 19

WHEN WE GOT TO the vehicles it was Eric who asked, "So where are we going?"

I frowned and counted up how many people we had. "We're going to have to take two cars. Ines and Jerrod, you come with me. Eric, you take the other car and follow us. We have to get to the other side of town before they realize we have figured them out."

Eric didn't seem to like my answer but did as I asked anyway.

Once in the car and on the road, Jerrod leaned between the front seats. "How did you find out where Michael is, anyway?"

As I came to a stop light, I contemplated if I should tell him. If father were here, he wouldn't be too happy to know I spread our business around to the other supernaturals. However, I did just tell all the shifters what was going on, so it was kind of a moot point.

"Xavier," I stated simply. "I told him a few days ago."

"And he found Michael already?" Ines questioned, and a glance at her face showed her suspicion. "How do you know it wasn't Xavier who took him in the first place?"

"Yeah," Jerrod added, "what she said."

I huffed and turned the wheel a bit more sharply than needed, throwing the two of them around in the car. "I don't, okay. To me this just proves what I said to my father was true. If we stopped all these secrets and who can be the strongest bullshi,t and worked together, we wouldn't have been in this situation in the first place. We could have found Michael days after he was taken, if not sooner."

"And he wouldn't have..." Ines trailed off, her voice wavering. She swallowed and I watched from the side of my eye as she got a hold of herself.

Good. She was holding up to her part of the deal. I didn't want to have to pull over and make her get out. Not when we were this close.

I slowed the vehicle down once we were close to the street Xavier had mentioned. Part of me hoped that he was there waiting for me, and the other part didn't want to see him. It would be easier if I didn't have to see him.

"You okay?" Ines asked, placing a hand on my leg.

I realized I'd stopped at a stop sign and hadn't gone when it was my turn. "Uh, yeah. Sorry, spaced for a second."

"Are you sure you two can handle this?" Jerrod asked from the back. "You two were the closest to Michael. It may not be a bad idea to stay out of this one."

"No," Ines and I said at the same time. Meeting each other's gaze, Ines and I nodded together, a knowing look passing between us.

"Alright, then. Don't bite my head off." he leaned to the side behind my seat. I assumed to look out the window. "Is this the place?"

I'd stopped the car a bit down from the building Xavier had told me to look. "No, just a bit further. We go by foot."

"Ugh," Jerrod complained as we got out of the vehicle. "What's the point of a car if we don't get to use them?"

I pursed my lips and gave him a look. "Do I really need to explain a covert operation to you?"

Eric and the others appeared next to us as Ines explained, "Don't mind him. He always complains when he has to do more than the bare minimum."

"Hey, I do more than the bare minimum." Jerrod scowled at her, and Ines twisted around to argue with him more.

"Are we going to go save Michael or fight here all day?" I reminded them of what we came here to do, and Ines and Jerrod promptly shut up, waiting for my instructions.

"Okay," I told them, trying to get a good look at the building from a block away. "The building is a little further up there. Most of these old buildings have more than one exit. So, me, Ines, and Jerrod can go through the front. Eric, you take the others around back. Try not to split up if you don't have to, they already got one of the best of us as it is."

Everyone had a solemn expression on their face after that. We walked in silence, the nervous tension getting to everyone. I still had my Colts unclasped from the meeting with the shifters and now as we grew closer to the building, I drew them, holding them at my sides.

I waved one in the direction of the alley between the two buildings for Eric and them to go before leading Ines and Jerrod to the front. Unlike the other buildings on the street this one's windows were boarded up, the glass broken out of each one of them. The paint was peeling along the sides and the door was barely hanging on to its hinges.

"How did we not think to check this place?" Jerrod murmured as we prepared to push the door open and duck inside. "I mean it's right by that bar he likes to frequent. We should have just put out bottles of booze and he would have come running home." Jerrod oofed and I figured Ines hit him over the head. Rightly so.

Signaling to be ready, I reached for the door and pushed it open. Pressed up against the side of the building, we waited for someone to come pouring out or shots to fire. After a moment when nothing happened, I lifted my Colts and darted into the entryway, sweeping the area with my guns.

"Clear," I called back quietly. Ines and Jerrod came in behind me, their own weapons drawn. Ines was more of a traditionalist choosing to use blades than guns, both of them up and ready to fight. Jerrod liked guns, like me. Except he liked the big ones. Shots guns preferably. They were too loud for my taste and only held a few rounds at a time. I'd stick with my Colts thank you very much.

The first room had a single light on which was curious for an abandoned building. The room was empty of any living being besides a few rodents and cockroaches. There were empty metal desks and piles of papers strewn around. A coffee cup still sat on top of one pile of papers.

Ines put her hand around the sides. "Still warm."

We all tensed and searched for the next door. Someone was here or had been a few minutes ago.

We didn't have to push this door open; it was already gaping wide, light pouring through the doorway. We inched toward it, ready for anyone to come out at us. I stepped over the rubble, my foot catching on something, and stumbled into the room. This room was different from the others. Fluorescent lights filled the room making it take a moment for my eyes to adjust.

"Crsyta, watch out!" Eric's voice called out just a second before I got punched in the face.

"Fuck," I grunted, blinking up at the attacker except they were gone. "That was a cheap shot you coward!"

"H...hello?"

My gaze shifted around the room until they fell on Michael lying on a metal table with a try of medical instruments next to him.

Michael's dark blonde hair had grown ragged over his shoulders and a dirty beard on his face. His one blue eye searched out the room from where they had him strapped down to the table. He might be awake but I wasn't sure how conscious he was. They could have drugged him or something to keep him complacent. His clothes were filthy and torn in several places. A closer inspection showed there were black lines marked along different parts of his body.

I swallowed thickly. Oh gods.

"Michael!" Ines cried out running over to the table despite the danger. "Oh, my gods, Michael." Ines looked over him, grabbing at his face to look at where his ear was missing and then the bloodied eyelid. Before finally lifting his right arm, holding the bandaged nub up to her face, crying as she ran it over her face. "I can't believe we found you Michael!'

Slowly moving closer to Michael, I kept my eyes out for the person who had wacked me. "Ines, I don't think you should be going all gaga over Michael just yet. There's someone here."

"Where?" Ines peered around the room, not seeing who I had come in contact with. While the room was brighter than all the others there was a lot of plastic sheeting hanging from the ceilings. Easy pickings for hiding places.

"Keep your eyes out," I told Eric and the others who had come in from the other way. "They're still here somewhere."

Everyone grew quiet until just the sound of Michael's labored breathing could be heard. I moved slowly through the plastic sheets, my ears listening to any slight movement in the rest of the room. There. To the left. A skittering of feet.

I whipped around toward the sound, pointing my Colts up in that direction. A dim shadow could be seen through the sheets. I aimed for it, shooting off my weapons in quick succession. The first few missed and then there was a grunt.

"I think I got him," I muttered out to Jerrod. "Come on." We slowly moved toward the direction the sound had come from. Nothing moved behind the flowing sheets and for a moment I thought I could relax. Then someone bolted through the sheets and out the door in the back of the room.

"I got him!" Eric called out, who was closest to the door, and chased the figure into the dark.

"Wait, no," I shouted after him, stepping toward the door for a second. "Don't run off on your own!"

"Crysta," Michael gasped out, making me pause. I struggled for a moment on whether I should follow Eric or stay here with my brother. Finally making a decision, I made my way back to my brother.

"What are you doing here? Why aren't you in school?"

I narrowed my eyes on him and whacked him on the shoulder. "Well, I would be if someone hadn't gone and got himself kidnapped. What the fuck, Michael? What happened to Gabriel wasn't enough of a warning about going off on your own? You had us worried sick."

"And by us she means me and Crysta," Ines filled in, giving the others a judgmental look. "The rest of them didn't give a fuck about you once Abraham said you were dead."

"Hey, we did too." Jerrod shoved between us. "We just...didn't have any leads to go on. But we swear we would have kept looking had we known where to look."

Michael waved him off. "It's f... fine." He coughed and cleared his throat. "Water?"

"Oh, yes. Here." I searched around trying to find something for him to drink. In our rush away from Arcadia we hadn't exactly prepared for everything.

"Here," Ines shoved something in Michael's face. A bottle. Michael drank from the bottle without question.

After chugging half the bottle, he belched and then coughed. "Whiskey. That's my girl." He grinned at Ines, who sighed in content.

"Was there anyone else in here with you?" I asked once he'd finished making moon eyes at Ines. "How many of them are there?"

Michael shook his head, blinking his one eye. "I don't know. There was only one-"

A shot rang out.

My head jerked toward the sound. Eric. The kidnapper.

"Crysta," Ines reached out for me.

I shook my head and started toward where Eric and the figure had gone too. "I have to check it out. We can't save Michael just to lose someone else."

Running toward the back, I skimmed the dim room. There was a metal cage off to one side, left wide open now. I supposed they kept Michael in there when they weren't cutting pieces of him off. I gritted my teeth and marched to the back room.

Eric stood over a form, his gun drawn and low to the ground.

I ran up beside Eric, my weapons drawn. They weren't needed. The guy was dead. He wasn't anything remarkable to look at. Just a regular guy with brown hair and a ruddy complexion. It wasn't anyone I knew.

"I think I got him." Eric stared at the man with a sort of surprised look on his face as if he couldn't believe he was the one who had killed him.

I knelt by the guy, noticing the place where I had hit him before. Just a graze on the shoulder. Fuck my aim was off. Eric's wasn't though. He'd hit the guy point blank in the forehead. I frowned at the scene before me. How had he done it? I didn't know Eric had such spot on aim. Especially not while aiming for a moving target...

"Did you get him?" Jerrod came up behind us out of breath, breaking me from my thoughts.

"No," I frowned, staring at Eric. "He did."

"Well," Jerrod smacked Eric on the back. "Good job. We can chalk one up for the good guys."

"Yeah," I murmured as Eric accepted the praise from our fellow Van Helsings.

"I'd have liked to question the guy before you killed him," I commented but no one was paying attention to me. They were too busy cooing over Michael and crowing over Eric's good shot.

"Oh, come on, Crysta." Jerrod smacked me on the back while I glowered over the body. "We found your brother and killed the bad guy. You owe your vampire lover a good blowie for this one."

"We broke up," I said offhandedly.

Jerrod frowned. "Oh, well then. Maybe you should get back together now that you're no longer the heir, eh?" He bumped me with his elbow, and I swatted him away. "Maybe not."

Ines appeared with Michael in tow behind her being helped by one of the others. "What are you doing hanging around here? Michael needs medical attention." Everyone stared at her for a moment, and she added with a growl, "Now!"

Then in a flurry of movement they were all helping her get Michael until there was someone on every arm and leg of him.

"Hey, I can walk you know." Michael griped as they marched him out of the back door. "I'm injured, not dead."

"Oh, shut up," Ines commanded. "Just let them give you a hand for once." Everyone froze at her words and even Ines winced.

Michael broke the awkward silence. "Speaking of hands...has anyone seen mine?"

CHAPTER 20

QUINN AND THE OTHER medic, Greg, weren't sure if they would be able to reattach Michael's...parts. Just thinking it made my stomach roll. However, my brother the trooper was always willing to be a guinea pig. Especially if it meant he'd be able to use both hands again. He didn't care so much about the ear.

"I think the eye patch makes me look roguish. Don't you?" Michael smirked at Ines who hadn't left his side since the moment we brought him home.

"Sure, it does." Ines rolled her eyes at him, smiling. Though, you could tell that she was ecstatic to have him home in any form that was alive.

"Yes, yes. We're all happy to have you back and well." My father smiled a proper smile for the first time since I'd been home. He stood at the end of Michael's bed fully dressed in his daily suit and tie, hands folded in front of him. "Now that you are here, we can focus on what is important. Of course, I would not expect you to take up your duties as heir right away."

"Father," I stepped in growling, "do you really think now is the time to be worrying about that?"

"We cannot be idle even at our worst," Abraham shot me a look before he gestured to Michael's prone form. "He will need time to recover, and I hear Quinn is very hopeful about reattaching your..." he cleared his throat. "Well, in any case, we can fake your hand until something permanent can be done about it. Your ear can be concealed by your hair." He scowled as he looked at Michael's face. "I suppose the patch is the best we can do for now."

"Yes," my brother pumped his fist at our father's approval of the patch but then his grin flattened out. "Actually, I'm not coming back to the clan."

"What?" I gaped at him. Everyone's heads turned in Michael's direction.

"I'm not going to be the heir," Michael repeated, then glanced at me with a small smile. "Sorry, sis. It's your job now."

"Don't speak nonsense," my father answered, waving Michael's words off dismissively.

"I'm not." Michael shook his head and then held Ines's hand tight staring down at the blankets. "While I was there, waiting to die, I made a promise to myself." He glanced up and scanned the room. "I have spent my whole life living for someone else. This clan, the supernaturals. I've never been out of the area or even seen the ocean."

"You have sacrificed for your family as any honorable heir would have," my father tried to placate him.

"Three hundred years," Michael stated. "Over three hundred years I have given to this family and now it's time to give back to myself. After I heal..." he took a deep breath and let it out, locking eyes with me. "I'm leaving."

"But what about Ines? You're to be married!" my father tried once more bringing Ines into it as a last-ditch effort.

Michael grinned at his fiancé. "Well, I kind of hoped she'd come with me."

Ines beamed at Michael and nodded, tears in her eyes. "Of course, I will. I don't want to ever lose you again."

"You cannot just -"

Michael interrupted father, "Yes, I can and I am. Either don't retire or let Crysta do it. Unless you have someone else in mind?"

My father pressed his lips firmly together as if he wanted to argue some more but the eyes in the room were too much for him. After a long moment, he finally said, "Very well. It seems that I will have no say in the matter. In any case, your sister seems to have quite the knack for handling the supernaturals." He turned his attention in my direction. "It would be a waste to lose all the ground you have covered already. Besides, the alpha seems quite taken with you."

My brows furrowed with confusion. "Uh, what?"

Father bobbed his head. "Oh, yes. He has requested a private audience with you to discuss more of this thing you want to start between them. Seems your stalking out to save your brother showed integrity and respect for your family. Something as you know the shifters value above all else."

"You mean besides the fact that I grabbed him by the balls?"

Michael threw his head back and laughed. "Oh, fuck. I wish I could have seen that."

Everyone else in the room retorted at once, "No, you don't."

"And the man of the hour, of course." My father turned to Eric, standing off to the side looking the part of humble hero. "If not for Eric's perfect timing and persistence then we would not be where we are today. A family again."

Eric feigned embarrassment, scratching the back of his neck. "I was just doing my duty. It could have been anyone."

"Now, now." My father walked over to him and clapped him on the back. "You have to take credit where it's due. We can't all claim to have saved one of our very own from a sadistic killer. We'll have to make sure you are amply rewarded."

"Well, I can't say no to that." Eric flushed with glee, beaming at my father.

"Wonderful. Come along and we'll discuss the details." My father ushered Eric from the room, not giving my brother another look.

"You'd think he'd be happier to see his son," Jerrod muttered next to me.

I snorted. "Are you kidding? That was Father happy."

"And what about you?" Jerrod murmured to me, so as not to draw my brother and Ines's attention. "Why aren't you happy to see him? You got what you wanted, right? Your brother is home and safe. All is right with the world."

"I know," I sighed and then shook my head. "It just feels wrong somehow. Like it was too easy, and Eric gets the kill?" My fingers curled into tight fists. "Just seeing that makes my blood boil."

"What do you have against him anyway?" Jerrod turned his head toward me. "He's been nothing but nice to you."

I shrugged. "He just bugs me. He's too damn happy."

Jerrod laughed and smacked me on the back, earning a glare from me. "I think you're getting cynical in your old age."

"Like you're one to talk. You're coming up on what? A hundred and five?" I poked him in the chest. "If anyone is old, it's you."

"You two seem like you're having fun. Want to share?" Michael called from his bed. One glance around the room showed that only Ines and us were left.

"Nah, I've got to get down to the kitchens." Jerrod pointed a thumb back at the door.

I grinned. "Ana still making you pay?"

Jerrod walked backward to the door and shrugged. "What can I say? I can't say no to her cooking."

I laughed as he dashed out the door. When he was gone, I turned back to my brother and my laughter sobered. Just seeing him lying there pissed me off. I didn't even get a chance to beat the shit out of whoever did this to him. The guy was dead before I ever got a word from him.

Damn it, Eric.

"Hey, now." Michael interrupted my thoughts. "What's with that look? I'm injured here, not dead."

Walking over to the end of the bed, I sat on the edge. "I know. Just wish we could have given that guy a taste of his own medicine. A bullet to the head was too easy a death."

"Tell me about," Ines smacked her fist into her hand, a wicked grin coming over her face. "I've dreamed of the ways I would torture the person who did this to my guy, and I feel a bit cheated too."

Inclining my head, I turned back to Michael. "I hear they're going to try and put your ear back on first. Are you excited?"

Michael arched a brow. "To get my wound cut back open and then my ear sewed back on? Uh, no. The ability to hear without everything sounding muffled? For sure. And if that means they'll be able to put my hand back on, then I'll take all the pain in the world for that."

Ines gripped the bandaged arm where my brother was missing a hand. She had taken it like a trooper this whole time, not once freaking out like she had at seeing his parts in boxes. I supposed she was trying to keep it together for Michael. He had enough to worry about without adding her to the mix.

"Hey, In," Michael reached out and placed his hand on top of her own. "Why don't you give me and my little sis a moment."

"But I -"

"You haven't eaten or showered since I got back and honestly," Michael crinkled his nose up. "You're starting to get a bit ripe."

Ines scowled at him. "Oh, whatever. Fine. I suppose I can take twenty minutes." She narrowed her eyes on Michael. "But that's it. I'm not letting you out of my sight ever again."

Michael laughed as she stalked out of the room. "A bit overprotective now, isn't she?"

I smiled. "Don't pretend you don't love it."

"I do." Then Michael's face sobered. "For a while there I thought I wasn't going to come back."

"I know. I'm sorry I didn't get to you sooner." I shifted closer to him on the bed.

Michael nodded. "I heard. Father can be a right bastard sometimes." I arched a brow and Michael laughed. "Okay, all the time. Still, you made up for it where it counts." He patted my thigh and grinned. "Who knows what they would have chopped off next?"

I smirked. "Worried about your favorite appendage?"

He pinched me on the thigh. "Hey, you would be too." He sighed and stared off to the side. "I didn't just send Ines away to have some bonding time. There's something I need to tell you."

I frowned and shifted closer. "What is it?"

"I haven't told father and don't plan on it. He'd just brush it off like he did my disappearance." His jaw tightened at that, showing for the first time how pissed off at our father he really was.

"I understand how you feel." I placed my hand on top of his and squeezed it. "I was furious when I found out that he had stopped searching. Then when the boxes started..." I trailed off and then swallowed, taking a breath before continuing, "Well, to say I was livid would be putting it lightly."

Michael squeezed my hand back. "And I appreciate it. I don't know what would have happened had you not pushed to find me." He stared off to the side for a long moment, a darkness in his eyes that had never been there before. "I was so alone. For so long. They'd bring me food occasionally just enough to keep me alive, not enough to ever be full."

I sat there and let him talk, knowing he needed to tell someone what happened to him.

He huffed a laugh. "I should have been grateful for those days. Just sitting there quietly in the dark, my grumbling stomach the only thing keeping me preoccupied. It would have been better than..." he glared down at his missing hand. "He knew me, Crysta." His eyes lifted to mine, angry tears shimmering there. "I don't know what he looked like, but I know his voice, his scent. He made sure to make the whole ordeal an intimate thing. Whispering in my ear all the horrible plans he had for me as if I were a loved one in bed with him. Fucking sick bastard."

I chewed on my lower lip not sure how to make him feel better. Pushing back my doubt, I gave a weak smile. "Hey, he's dead now. So, whatever he was, he's a dead bastard now."

Michael's eyes jerked to mine, locking onto them. "No. No, he's not."

My brows furrowed. "What do you mean?"

Shaking his head, Michael dragged his hand through his hair. "That man, the shifter, I don't know who he was, but it wasn't him."

"How do you know?"

Michael's smile was anything but nice. "They kept me for months, Crysta. I might have been starving but I do know how to count. There wasn't just one of them. There at least four and the one Eric got didn't smell right. He didn't smell like the guy who..." his voice choked up as Ines rushed back into the room, a towel around her body and a shower cap on her head.

Standing up, I let them be alone. I had a lot to think about and even more to plan.

I didn't bother to ask when Michael had the chance to smell the guy, but I took his words for it. What he was saying confirmed what I had been thinking all along. We hadn't gotten him. This wasn't over and whoever did this to him, to us, wasn't going to stop. They'd come for us again. This time we'd be ready for them.

ABOUT THE AUTHOR

Erin Bedford is an otaku, recovering coffee addict, and Legend of Zelda fanatic. Her brain is so full of stories that need to be told that she must get them out or explode into a million screaming chibis. Obsessed with fairy tales and bad boys, she hasn't found a story she can't twist to match her deviant mind full of innuendos, snarky humor, and dream guys.

On the outside, she's a work from home mom and bookbinger. One the inside, she's a thirteen-year-old boy screaming to get out and tell you the pervy joke they found online. As an ex-computer programmer, she dreams of one day combining her love for writing and college credits to make the ultimate video game!

Until then, when she's not writing, Erin is devouring as many books as possible on her quest to have the biggest book gut of all time. She's written over thirty books, ranging from paranormal romance, urban fantasy, and even scifi romance.

Come chat me up!
www.erinbedford.com
Facebook.com/erinrbedford
twitter.com/erin_bedford
Don't forget to follow me on Goodreads, Pinterest, Instagram, and TikTok!